A TOWN CALLED
TROUBLESOME

Matt Matthews had carved his ranch out of the wild Wyoming frontier. But he had his troubles. The big blow of '86 was catastrophic, with dead beeves littering the plains, and the oncoming winter presaged worse. On top of this, a gang of desperadoes had moved into the Snake River valley, killing, raping and rustling. All Matt can do is to take on the killers single-handed. But will he escape the hail of lead?

JOHN DYSON

A TOWN
CALLED
TROUBLESOME

Complete and Unabridged

LINFORD
Leicester

First published in Great Britain in 1998 by
Robert Hale Limited
London

First Linford Edition
published 1999
by arrangement with
Robert Hale Limited
London

British Library CIP Data

Dyson, John, *1943 –*
    A town called Troublesome.—Large print ed.—
Linford western library
    1. Western stories
    2. Large type books
    I. Title
    823.9'14 [F]

    ISBN 0–7089–5430–8

Published by
F. A. Thorpe (Publishing) Ltd.
Anstey, Leicestershire

Set by Words & Graphics Ltd.
Anstey, Leicestershire
Printed and bound in Great Britain by
T. J. International Ltd., Padstow, Cornwall

This book is printed on acid-free paper

1

Sundown Jack knelt among the night-time shadows of sugar pines that swathed the sides of the Wyoming valley and studied the Matthews ranch. The lamp that lit the bunkhouse, set back behind the pony corral, had gone out. It was early to bed and early to rise for those 'punchers. And now the hurricane lamp glimmering from the front window of the rancher's cabin was extinguished too. They were all hitting the hay. It was time to make his move.

The half-breed's dark face was impassive but his eyes glinted his resolve as his belly rumbled with hunger. He hadn't had a bite to eat all day. No time to pause to shoot game when a posse was on your heels. And those other varmints, too. He needed food and supplies, or

whatever they had to offer. Most of all he needed bullets for his Colt Frontier. He had used all his in an exchange of leaden compliments with the lawmen and with his one-time friends.

Sundown was a young man of mixed race, his mother a Sioux squaw, his father a French trapper. He was attired in a mixture of Indian and cowboy clothes, fringed leather trousers and moccasins, a red wool shirt, and white man's suit jacket. From beneath his high-crowned Stetson, his black hair hung to his shoulders, pinned back from his brow by a beaded headband.

He waited a while longer to let them settle down, then stood and loose-hitched his liver-and-cream pinto to a bough. 'At least there don't seem to be no dogs,' he muttered. 'You wait here Smoke, this ain't gonna take me long.' He figured there was some kind of lean-to store alongside the cabin. It looked easy enough to break into.

Sundown Jack picked his way across the mountainside, silent as a wraith.

When he reached a cliff of shale he slithered down and landed lightly on the plank roof of the lean-to. He looked about him in the moonlight, intently listening. There was no sound apart from the distant howl of a pack of wolves in full cry out hunting along the valley. He carefully prised up two planks with his long Bowie knife, eased them free and dropped down inside. Of smallish stature, he was as lean and agile as a cat. He struck a match and saw a side of bacon hanging from a hook. He cut himself a slice and chewed it down as he searched around. Whoever lived here had a good housekeeper. There were neatly arranged barrels of flour, molasses, nuts, baking powder, and other dried goods, with smoked meats and fish dangling on hooks about his head. Sundown filled his mouth and pockets with whatever he fancied and tossed the bacon-side out on to the roof for later consumption.

He found a candle stub on a holder

and by its glow saw boxes of nails, coils of rope and tools. There surely were bullets somewhere . . .

★ ★ ★

Matt Matthews had just made love to his wife, Mary, on the pile of bearskins that served as their bed, trying not to make overmuch sound that might disturb their seven-year-old son, Jed, sleeping in his adjacent cubby-hole. Suddenly he heard a scraping sound and his horny hand tensed on her pale breast as their eyes clinched in the candlelight. Her face was flushed as she looked up at him, anxiously. 'What is it?'

'Sounds like some critter's got into the store shed,' he whispered. 'Most likely that raccoon agin.'

'It's not that bear?'

'Nope,' he smiled, disentangling himself from her and reaching for his rifle. 'He'd be making a durn sight more noise than that.'

Mary modestly pulled her nightdress together to cover herself as she sat up. 'Matt,' she hissed. 'Take care.'

He nodded silently, hauling up his long johns, standing tall and broad-shouldered. He parted a sacking curtain and peered through at his son. In sleep the boy had all the innocence of childhood, one arm thrown back, his long fair hair fallen across his eyes. 'He's sleeping,' he whispered.

Matt thumbed back the hammer of the Winchester and eased a slug into the breech. He carefully raised the latch of the bedroom door and stepped out into the dark living-room. He skirted the stove and listened at the store-room door. Yes, there was something, or someone, in there sure enough. As stealthily as an Indian he slipped back the bolt inch by inch until he could push the door open with his bare foot.

'Shee-it!' Sundown Jack heard the creak of the door too late as it swung open and he froze, his hand tightening on his knife. He felt the cold steel of a rifle barrel on the back of his neck. 'Howdja sneak up on me like that?'

'Jest drop that knife, you lousy thievin' skunk, 'fore I blow your head clean off your shoulders.' Matt, with his spare hand, slipped the revolver from the 'breed's holster. 'An' I'll have this, too.'

Sundown Jack tossed the Bowie clattering away. 'OK, boss. Fair deal. Don't do anythin' fool-headed now. I'm only borrowin' a bit of grub, was planning on payin' you back.'

'Like hell you was,' Matt growled.

'Didn't want to disturb you folks seein' as how you'd gone to bed.'

'Who is he? What's going on?'

Sundown Jack turned at the sound of the woman's voice and his savage countenance split into a grin when he saw her standing in the doorway in her nightdress, her blonde hair tumbled down about her shoulders.

'Jest payin' a social call, missis. Thought you might lend me some vittles. I'm hungry, you see. Real hungry. I come a long way.'

'A dirty sneakin' thief in the night, that's what you are. I'm gonna hand you over to the law.'

'Sure, boss, that's your right, I guess. Didn't mean to disturb your slumbers,' Jack grinned. 'Or whatever it was you was doing.'

Mary felt herself blushing as the dark eyes burned insolently and coolly up and down over her, assessing her body. She pulled the cotton nightdress more tightly to her throat, but that only accentuated the firmness of her breasts. There was something about the half-Indian that both frightened and upset her. Something about the amusement in his eyes, his lack of fear, although Matt had the rifle jammed to his chest.

'Mighty purty white gal squaw you got there, mistuh,' the 'breed drawled. 'If she hadn'ta bin I guess you'da bin fast asleep by now and wouldn't have heard me. Eh?'

'You shut your dirty mouth. Mary, get some rope. We're tying this boy up.'

'Sure, boss. Tie me real tight. Take me into Oglala and they'll hang me by the throat. But you cain't stop me sayin' that I sure know you're the lucky one for havin' such a handsome gal. Where you find her? She sure ain't from round here.'

Matt raised the rifle as if to smash him in the face with the butt. 'You need to be taught some respect.'

'Sure, all us 'breeds need that. What do I care if tomorrow my heels gonna be kickin' air?'

'Mary, where's that rope?'

'Is it — ?' She paused, staring at her husband, the anger on his gaunt face. 'Is it necessary? If he's hungry? Can't we let him take some food and go on his way? I'm sure he wasn't planning to harm us.'

'No, missis, I sure wasn't.'

'Come on, Mary, he's broken into our home. Don't go thinking he's just

8

some poor wild starving animal who can't help his ways.'

'No more I can, boss, that's true.'

'It's pretty obvious he's some damn outlaw on the lam. Probably a rustler. We've gotta hand him over.'

'Aw, come on, boss. Do as your missis says. Gimme a chance.'

'If you were a decent man you should have knocked on our door and we would have fed you,' Mary said. 'Isn't that so?'

Sundown Jack held her gaze. 'If thet's so you must be like one of them Bible pictures the mission lady has. All that hair like sunburned corn and them eyes blue as the sky. Must be an angel come down to earth.'

'That's enough,' Matt said, uncomfortably. 'I ain't standing here in my long johns all night palaverin' with you.'

'Waal, who in hell would give food to a 'breed in these parts?' Jack snarled.

'We would,' Mary said. 'Come on, Matt. Bring him inside. We can be

Christian about this.'

'Jeesis!' Matt breathed. 'If you say so.'

He followed them into the living-room, lighting the hurricane lamp, making sure he kept their visitor's revolver in his belt. Mary poked some life into the fire of the stove to warm up a pot of stew. She buttoned on an old greatcoat of Matt's to make herself more decent and straightened her hair.

'Siddown,' Matt growled. 'What's your handle?'

'Sundown Jack.'

The rancher glanced at him sharply. 'Not *the* Sundown Jack?'

'Guess that's me.'

'The rodeo rider? The one who won the big cross-country race up in Montana last year?'

'Uhuh.'

'I heard about yuh. Whadja do with all that prize money?'

'What do you think, boss? I got into bad company. Bad whiskey, bad poker

10

games, bad girls. Soon goes.'

'So what you doin' in these parts?'

'Thet bad company I tol' you 'bout. Why, thanks, missis.' Sundown Jack took the bowl of stew Mary placed before him, and appraised her, admiringly, before he began to spoon it down. 'Me an' them parted company awhile back.'

Matt eyed him, sternly. 'Would they be that gang of cut-throats who were run out of Montana by the vigilantes?'

'Some folks called them that. I ain't with 'em no more, boss.'

'I had an idea they were headin' this way. Hell's teeth. Where are they?'

'Like I said, we parted company back along the Snake River. I didn't cotton to their ways.'

'What happened?'

Jack pushed the cleared plate away, glanced at Mary and said, significantly, 'It ain't something I want to talk about. Not in front of the lady.'

'Bad, eh?' Matt rolled the makings of a cigarette as Mary placed mugs of

11

coffee before them. 'Come on, we're being fair with you; you be straight with us.'

'I use the pipe.' Jack pulled a stonebowled Indian one from his coat pocket. 'Maybe we can talk peace.'

'Help yourself.' Matt pushed the tobacco pouch over. 'Just tell us what's been going on.'

The 'breed's nimble fingers stuffed tobacco into the bowl and he took his time lighting up. 'What I mean is, I was there but I didn't take no part. If I talk, you ain't gonna haul me in on this?'

'Give. You got my word.'

'Waal,' Sundown drawled, 'I ain't got nuthin' against a li'l rustlin'. But when it comes to what they did to that ferryman's missis after they kilt him, I draw the line.'

'What did they do?' Mary asked, firmly.

'They had their fun. You know what I mean? Then they scalped her. Thass when me and them fell out.'

'Oh, my God!' Mary sank down on to a chair, clutching the overcoat to her, staring at the half-Indian. 'Why? Poor woman. Who was she? Where?'

'Along the Snake River. Johnson's Crossing. That was his moniker. He was the ferryman. They both dead.'

'Who did it?' Matt thundered. 'That's more to the point.'

Sundown Jack let smoke trickle from his hawklike nostils, put the pipe down. 'No names, boss. I tell you that I'se a dead man. It's against the code.'

'What code?' Mary asked.

'He means a perverted kinda thieves' honour. They don't split.'

'Thass right, boss. I don't split. Not even if I ain't ridin' with 'em no more.'

For moments they lapsed into silence, staring into their own thoughts, listening to the eerie howl of the wolves along the valley. 'Them devils are after my herd,' Matt muttered, fingering his rifle.

'There's gonna be more than wolves

after your herd, mistuh. You can count on that.'

'What do you mean?' Mary asked, alarmed.

'He means these cut-throat friends of his.'

'Waal, much as I like you folks, guess I gotta be on my way.' Jack knocked out the pipe, finished his coffee and got to his feet. 'I got my pinto waitin' on the hillside. If you'd jest hand me back my Frontier.'

Matt, who had pulled on some britches and a shirt, eyed him, severely. 'I'll ride with you a ways. See you off my property.'

'Waal.' Sundown Jack grinned foolishly, and began to empty the capacious pockets of his tattered jacket of nuts and other goodies. 'Guess I gotta return these.'

'Aw, keep what you got,' Matt shrugged, getting his boots on. 'Ought to make you mend the hole in the roof 'fore you go.'

'There's a side of bacon on top.

Don't s'pose you got six bullets to spare? I plumb run out.'

'No, I ain't. Never met a 'breed with so much durn cheek.'

Jack's smile left his face as he heard the sound of horses' hoof-falls outside in the night.

'Hello the house,' a voice called.

'Who the hell's that?' Matthews stepped over to the small window and peered out at the shadowy shapes of horsemen in the yard. 'Fine time of night to come callin'.'

'It's either them or t'others,' the 'breed hissed. 'Either way I'm gonna need me a gun. Come on, mistuh. Let me make a run for it.'

'There's too many of 'em. You'd never make it.' Matt could see only men in tall hats, bandannas up across their mouths, in long riding coats or mackinaws, their mustangs prancing and frothing at the bit. For seconds he knew a cold emptiness inside at the thought they might be the Montana bunch. 'Nope.' He shouted with relief as he caught sight of a tin star pinned to a lanky rider's coat. 'It's Luke Hanlon. Sheriff at Oglala.'

Sundown Jack looked wildly around, backing away to the store-room door and for the first time Mary saw fear in his eyes.

'It's no good,' Matt said. 'They got you surrounded.'

'Shee-it!' Sundown groaned, once more. 'More fool me.'

Matt unbarred the door and stepped out on to the porch, holding the lantern aloft. 'Howdy, boys,' he shouted. 'I jest heard about the trouble at Johnson's Crossing. That what you on?'

'Who you heard from?' Luke Hanlon, his onetime deputy when he was lawman at Oglala, peered down at him.

'Friend of mine, Sundown Jack. He's inside. No need for those guns, boys. Step down. Come on in.'

★ ★ ★

Luke Hanlon had a long-jawed face and country-boy ways. He was as tall as Matthews, but in a gangling, gawky sort of way. He was no hot-shot, no match for any gun-slinging dude if it came to a duel. But he was upright and honest and the only man who had applied for the job. So sheriff he was. 'Evenin', Mary,' he mumbled, touching his hat. 'Sorry to burst in on you like this.'

He was toting his carbine just in case of trouble and he had it pointed at the 'breed as the six members of his posse came stomping in behind him, packing the small cabin space. 'That's him. He's one of 'em.'

'Howdy, boys,' Sundown Jack grinned recklessly, as the men roughly grabbed hold of him, twisting his arms behind his back with a force that made him wince. 'You sheriff at Oglala? Jest the man I'm lookin' for.'

'You bet I am. An' I'm the man who's gonna be tyin' a rope around your neck.'

'Steady on, boys,' Matthews growled, trying to restrain them. 'I know your feelin's, but this fella's already given hisself up to me. He reckons he weren't no part of it.'

'You ain't lawman now, Matt. I'm sheriff an' I'll take care of this. This bastard tried to kill us with his rifle fire. We bin on his trail all day.'

'If I'd wanted to kill you, you wouldn't be here now,' Sundown gasped, as one held him by the throat and twisted his head back by the hair.

'Please, gentlemen, this is my house,' Mary shouted. 'He's not going to try to escape. Leave him be.'

It was obvious if she hadn't been there the 'breed would have received a severe beating and maybe been strung up there and then. But the folks thereabouts were somewhat in awe of the pretty, well-spoken blonde girl from the East, who had visited Oglala on a lecture tour with her father and stayed to marry the then sheriff. So, they quietened down, shuffling and murmuring.

'Doncha worry, Mary,' Luke drawled. 'This varmint's gonna git a fair trial, then we'll hang him.'

'Iffen you do that,' Sundown said, 'you won't find the kid.'

'You what?' This started a new outbreak of threats and grabbing at him, like a pack of dogs about to tear him to pieces. 'You know where she is?'

'Sure I know. I took her, didn't I?'

'What you done to her?' Hanlon reached out for his throat, his rifle raised to buffalo him. 'Where is she, you lousy cur?'

'She's safe. But 'less I get a deal I ain't talkin'. You'll never find her.'

This aroused another howl of threats and insults, as Matt tried to calm them. 'What you talkin' about?'

'The Johnsons. Both slaughtered. They had a five-year-old girl. She's missing.'

'Is that so?' Matt pondered on this. 'I think what Sundown Jack did was rescue her from those cut-throats. I can tell you, you beat him to pulp he ain't a man who's gonna break. Mebbe you owe him an apology?'

'An apology?' Luke's face was shrill with indignation. 'Only apology he'll git is at the end of a rope.'

'Come on, Luke. It makes sense. What matters is to get that li'l gal back. And the only way is to offer him a deal.'

'Deal? With him?'

'Yeh. An' I reckon that means his freedom.'

'His freedom? Are you crazy? He's one of 'em. He shot at us. Led us a crazy ride all across country. Helped the others get away.'

At this point young Jed woke up and entered the room, sleepy-eyed, in his night-shirt, to find out what all the shouting was about. 'What's going on, Pa?'

'Nuthin'. You stay with your mother.

Come into the other room a minute, Luke.'

When they had some privacy, he said, 'Look, Luke, you're sheriff now and I don' want to interfere. This man admits he did some rustling, but I believe him when he says he didn't go along with those boys' dirty ways. He knows who they are. He won't give no names but maybe, who knows, maybe he can help us. He's a loner, wild for sure, but I figure he's decent underneath. I'm ready to vouch for him. I'll give him a job on the ranch. You could kinda put him on parole. Have a word with the judge. But we gotta act fast if we gonna find that child.'

'You reckon?' Luke scratched his long jaw. 'Yeah, I see what you mean, Matt. I guess you're right.'

'You woulda figured it out for yourself if you weren't so riled up. An' who can blame you after what you seen?'

'Yeah, it weren't a pretty sight. Those

men gotta be stopped.'

Luke strolled back into the room. 'Boys, Mistuh Matthews here has offered the loan of fresh horses. If Sundown Jack leads us to where the Johnson girl is and she's unharmed I've decided to parole him.'

'She with Sioux friends. She not be hurt. Whadja mean, parole?'

'You'll have to work for Mistuh Matthews here for a while until the judge decides. OK? You willing to abide by that?'

'Suits me.' Sundown Jack smiled at Mary. 'Suits me just fine.'

2

It was the fall of the year and already the air had the bite of winter. There had been a heavy snow overnight, blocking the high passes, but the wind had dropped and the sky was a clear, crystal blue. Matt Matthews led the riders back into his ranch holding the little girl, Lucy Johnson, snuggled into his bearskin coat. She was a pert child, large eyes beneath a bundle of curls, and seemed none the worse for her experience except she kept asking when she was going home to her Mama and Pa. Nobody had found the words to tell her she wouldn't be seeing them again.

'Put my broncs in the corral, boys. Your own should be rested up enough to git you back to Oglala. An' come on in for breakfast.'

They had ridden half the night on

fresh horses supplied by Matt. Sundown Jack had led the way on his fleet, sure-footed little pinto, Smoke, along hardly perceivable trails through the dense pine woods, climbing steadily up into the mountains until they reached a stream-fed clearing Matt had never come across before. There were a few stunted ponies and three tattered tipis. Sundown Jack had gone ahead and emerged with a Sioux Indian, in buckskins and blanket, who had the child asleep in his arms. The men went forward watched by a huddle of solemn-faced warriors, squaws and children as the girl was handed over.

'What these people doin' here?' Luke had demanded. 'They oughta be on the reservation.'

'Looks like they missed the army dragnet,' Matt had replied for, after the Custer massacre, all Indians had been cleared out of the area. 'It's my land. I ain't got no objection to 'em being here.'

He had had a short pow-wow with

these remnants of a once-strong Oglala tribe, many of them showing scars of war, a now beaten people. 'This is my land, but I trust you. You leave my cows alone you can stay here.' He had rewarded them with tobacco and left them.

Mary came out to greet them and reached up to take Lucy. 'Why, she's a cute little thing,' she said, wistfully. 'You come on inside.'

Sundown Jack hung back, jumping lightly down, an arm around the neck of his exhausted pinto, the dark eyes in their slits glancing at the men, and across at the freedom of the hills. He was obviously concerned whether they were going to keep their word.

Matt saw his air of tension and grinned. 'Guess we owe Jack our thanks, Luke. You can put the pinto in the stable, Sundown. You'll find a spare bed in the bunkhouse. We could all do with some rest.'

Jack smiled crookedly, noting that he wasn't being asked to join the others in the rancher's cabin. 'Sure, boss.'

After Mary had fed the men and they were sat around wherever they could find space sucking at mugs of hot coffee, she hugged the little girl to her and asked, 'Where will she go?'

'Town council will pay to board her at Widow Macey's house 'til we hear whether she's any relatives,' Luke said.

'But what if she hasn't, poor little mite?'

'In that case,' Luke muttered, 'she'll be sent back to Omaha to the orphanage.'

'What you gonna do about them who killed her ma and pa, Luke?' Matt asked.

'Waal — ' Luke stroked his long unshaven jaw uncomfortably. 'Seems to me they've headed on down the Snake. That's out of my jurisdiction, Matt, you know that. If them killers got any sense they'll keep on travellin' right outa this territory.'

'And if they haven't?'

'They show their mangy faces along this valley again, you send me word.'

Matt looked troubled. 'Maybe I won't have time.'

'What more can I do? I got taxes to collect, work to do in town. These boys got their homes to go to, their farms to run.'

'Yeah, true. Tomorrow I'll head out along the valley, see if there's any traces of 'em. I'm worried about my cows.'

'You catch any of them scumbags you bring 'em in. We'll hang 'em.' Luke got to his feet, eager to be on his way, reaching out for the child. 'Come on, Lucy, say goodbye to Missis Matthews now. You comin' with me.'

'Don't want to,' Lucy moaned, clinging to Mary.

'Sure you do.' Luke extricated her and bundled her under his arm. 'So long, Mary. So long, Matt. Come on, boys.'

They stood and watched them canter out, and Mary clutched Matt's arm.

'Couldn't we . . . couldn't we take her, if she's got no one?'

Matt glanced anxiously up at the sky, at the white fangs of the Snake mountains to the north. 'Only mid-November and the first snow. If we get the same blizzards as last winter I'll be finished, Mary, you know that.'

★ ★ ★

John Dog Crandal sat his horse on a wooded rise looking down at the meandering Snake River which went bubbling and frothing through icy banks. He was a lean and hungry-looking man, his shoulders hunched in a worn frock coat, his wolfish face encased in a black beard beneath a wide-brimmed hat. The object of his attention was a bunch of longhorns at a more shallow loop of the river. They were nosing forward trying to drink and scrambling back as the ice broke beneath them. John Dog looked around at his men, the scum of the Montana mining camps, Slippery Williams, Hambone Jones, Snake Eyes Finnegan, Seedy Smith, and the greaser, Emmanuel Estevez, also known as the Knife Man. They had mugged and killed drunken miners, looted stage coaches and gold consignments until the populace had turned against them and the vigilantes had chased them out of the country. They had drifted south through Wyoming causing mayhem. It was John Dog's proud boast that they were more feared than the James gang.

He gave a thin-lipped grin at them and drawled, 'I sure could eat me a six-inch steak.' He raised his Kentucky longarm, an old-fashioned muzzle-loader, but one he swore by for accuracy, winding its leather strap tight around his firing wrist. He aimed at a full-grown cow. The buckhorn sight was set on the front bead at a point behind the cow's right shoulder. He adjusted slightly for distance and to take account of the strong wind, knowing the rifle like an old friend. He squeezed off a ball and the report echoed and clattered across the mountain face. The cow gave a bellow and collapsed to her knees, blood foaming, her eyes rolling as she toppled to her side and lay still. Shot through the heart at 300 yards. The rest of the herd swung their wide horns, looking around them wildly, and set off as one accord bounding away along the riverbank, their tails crooked high, moaning their anger and fear as they kicked up snow.

'Leave 'em. They'll soon settle. We'll catch up, shoot some more.'

'What we shootin' 'em fer?' Slippery asked, for to a dyed-in-the-wool rustler like him it seemed a wasteful practice when they could drive them to a market.

'Because we are. We'll skin the hides and load up that ferryman's buggy with raw meat. We'll take it into Troublesome to sell. That way nobody gits to see the brands. I weren't born yesterday.'

Behind his back Slippery raised a crooked finger to tap at his temple and raised his eyebrows at Hambone. 'How'd we git mixed up with this crazy 'coon?' he muttered. But John Dog was already ploughing down the slope so they dug in their spurs and went charging after him.

When they reached the slain cow John Dog jumped down, pulled his long knife and slashed at the beast. Slippery shook his head as he watched. He was slow-elking her, taking only the hindquarters, leaving the rest of the valuable beast to freeze solid in the snow. John Dog tied the bloody meat to dangle each side at the back of his saddle. When his bronc whinnied and shied away from the smell of blood Crandal cuffed her hard across the nose. 'Damn you, hold still,' he shouted. 'You lousy piece of crowbait.'

'Ain't you takin' the rest?' Slippery asked.

'No, I ain't.' Crandal breathed hard with the effort of cutting away the

31

hide with the big MM of the brand, Matthews' ranch. 'You can, if you want. I'm hungry, thassall. Like I said, we'll go back to that ferryman's house, pick up his wagon, then we'll start slaughterin' for real.'

'Aw, do we have to go back there?' Slippery asked.

'What's the matter, scared of ghosts?'

'Naw, ain' thet. But that posse might still be around.'

'They've gawn.' John Dog grunted, rolling up the hide, tying it behind his saddle, and wiping his bloodstained hands in the snow. 'You saw 'em go. Sundown Jack drew 'em off.'

'Why'd he snatch the kid, why'd he light out like that an' take shots at us?' Hambone growled.

'Mebbe he's plannin' on gittin' a ransom for her. Sundown ain't stupid. Not like you dunkheads. Anyway he did us a favour. They went after him. And it ain't likely they'll be back jest yet. He'll lead 'em a merry dance.'

'I don't trust that 'breed,' Seedy

Smith whined. 'He never joined in the fun.'

'Boys, he wouldn't dare doublecross me. Nobody would. Anybody does he's a dead man.' John Dog hoisted himself back into the saddle, pulled on his gloves. 'Less go git thet wagon.'

When they reached the ferryman's cabin they approached carefully, but it had a forlorn, deserted air. The mule that provided the power of the ferry paddle was standing idle as if wondering where everybody had gone. There was a fine pair of wagon horses in the field. And in one corner the snowy mounds of two fresh graves, with makeshift crosses.

'Aw, ain't that sweet?' Slippery grinned. 'They done buried 'em.'

They harnessed the pair to the wagon and went off in search of longhorns. The rest of the day they spent shooting down some prime beasts and slaughtering them, uncaring whether they were bulls, steers, or cows with calves. They didn't give up until the wagon was groaning under the piled-up weight of the carcasses.

'Boys,' Crandal shouted to his assorted ruffians. 'I'm going back to the ferryman's cabin tonight. I sure am tired of sleeping out under the stars. Fancy me a little comfort. Nobody ain't gonna disturb us.'

They crowded into the cabin when they got back, built up a roaring fire and stuffed themselves on roasted steaks and flapjacks. As they sprawled about, burping and scratching at themselves, and passing the ferryman's whiskey jug, Crandal stretched out his long legs as he took pride of place in the rocking chair, before the blaze, and said, 'You boys can head on with the wagon downriver in the mornin'. Me an' Hambone will circle back, see what's happened to Sundown Jack or if anyone's followin'. OK, Hambone?'

The fat, shaven-headed young man, with forearms and fists like hambones protruding from his chequered shirt, grunted dully. 'Yuh.' His proven method of dealing with troublemakers was to give them one hammer blow on the crown of their heads, which probably accounted for his nickname. It generally put the recipient into oblivion. 'Sure, John Dog. I go with you.'

Crandal carefully tipped powder from his belthorn into the pan of his Kentucky, took a lead ball from his pouch and thrust it down the forty-inch barrel, using the detachable ramrod. He checked the flint was held firmly, and raised the longarm and squinted along the sights. 'If Sundown Jack has run out on us it's the last thing he'll ever have done.'

'Yuh,' Hambone agreed. 'The last thing.'

'We'll take a look at that rancher's place while we're at it. I like to know what the opposition's up to. We'll meet you boys back along the Snake at the fork with the Little Snake.'

'What you don' show?' Estevez drawled, idly flicking his rawhide bullwhip at the fire. 'Eez gonna be dangerous hangin' 'bout with thees stolen meat. What the rancher show before you?'

'What you do?' Crandal shouted. 'You kill him, thass what you do.'

'I say we head on for Troublesome,' the Mexican persisted. 'We got wagon. We travel slow. You easy catch up.'

'An' I say I'm givin' orders in this outfit, not some damn dago. You all wait where I tell you.'

'Sure.' The others nodded their assent. 'You're boss.'

John Dog swung the longarm to prod its dangerous end at the Mexican's throat. 'Is that agreed?'

The Mexican stared at him, venomously, slowly pushed the barrel aside. 'Like you say.'

'Yeah, so pass that jug.'

'Well, let's see, how far is it to Troublesome, my foine sorr?' Snake Eyes Finnegan had a heavy Irish burr. He was a flame-haired former sergeant in the Union cavalry before being discharged following some fraudulence to do with the quartermaster's stores. Since then he had ridden on the other side of the law. He still wore his faded forage cap with its badge. 'And what would we be doin' when we get there?'

'We would be after havin' ourselves a foine time in the saloons and the whorehouses,' Crandal mimicked. 'On the proceeds of these beeves. That's what we'd be doin'.'

'It's about four days' ride,' the black-toothed Slippery put in. 'It's a hell-hole of a town is Troublesome. You can buy and sell anything. Wish I'd brought my ole granny along. Could probably have got a price for her.'

'That's true.' Crandal smiled, as the men laughed. 'Hear tell there ain't a lot of law in Troublesome. Sounds like our sort of town, don't it, boys?'

3

It was a grey first light and snow a thin, crisp layer on the ground when Matt came out of the cabin. He jammed his Stetson over his nose, buttoned his bearskin coat, and held his rifle in his gloved hand. When he looked over at the corral he was surprised to see the shadowy figure of Sundown Jack. It was like he was whispering to the horses. They were a wild bunch of mustangs but he had coaxed them to him and seemed to be having a pow-wow.

'You sure got the magic touch,' Matt growled, his boots crunching on the snow as he approached. 'Generally these fellows take some catching.'

The 'breed turned his muddy eyes to the rancher, fondling a horse's nose as he slipped on a bridle. 'Most men don't know how to treat 'em.'

'Hear tell you're a pretty good wrangler.'

'I got my methods. Don't see any reason to halfkill 'em.'

'What about the rodeo? Those horses are treated real mean.'

Sundown shrugged. 'Thass white man's sport. Me, I only ride for money.'

'And mebbe you like the challenge?'

Jack grinned. 'Mebbe.'

'Couldn't you sleep?'

'Mistah, I don't like being closed in.'

'Don't blame you. Not with them two smelly galoots. They still snoring?'

'Yeah. We ridin' out? I'll git these four saddled. Give my paint a rest. This dun OK for you?'

'Sure. He ain't my usual but he'll do. We'll head west along the Snake see if there's any sign of them killers, them former friends of yourn. There's a line cabin at Dead Man's Creek, thirty miles along. That more or less marks the end of my range. We'll stay there tonight. How many of them *are* there?'

'Aw,' Sundown shrugged 'Five or six last count.'

'Well, there's four of us.'

'They're hard men. Expert shootists. Them two in the bunkhouse are no match for 'em.'

'We'll see.' Matt strode over to the low-pitched bunkhouse with its sod roof, booted open the door and hollered, 'Come on you lazy buckaroos. Outa them pits. We gotta go check on the herd.'

Old Caleb sat up in his filthy long johns rubbing his rheumy eyes. 'What in hell time is it?'

'Near sun-up. If we can see to ride we gonna ride. OK?'

'OK by me, boss. What about breakfast?'

'Mary's cooking it.' She wouldn't have Caleb in the cabin on account of his odour. He wouldn't be taking his annual bath until the thaw. 'Git up and go git it.'

40

'Fair enough. Where did I put my dang teeth?'

The other cowhand, Elijah, was still hanging on to his blanket pulled over his head as though a few more minutes' sleep was essential to him. Matt prodded him hard with the rifle. 'Wakey, wakey, you lousy bum. You'll have plenty time to sleep when you're dead.'

In the wake of the disastrous winter past he could barely afford to keep the two men on. Most other small ranchers paid off their hands with the onset of winter, setting them adrift to fend for themselves. Matt had had to let four men go. They would drift back to town, exist on odd jobs or handouts, or find work in the Cheyenne cattle pens. It would be easy enough to get new boys for the spring round-up and the summer cattle trail. But Caleb knew more about cows than most men in Wyoming and it would be foolish to lose him. Elijah was a solid young man, if a trifle dim, who could make a fair fist of most jobs. So he kept them on, for in these parts you could never be sure what roughnecks you might mistakenly hire.

Matt had a theory that most cows died in the dreadful blizzards that swept down from the north because nobody tried to save them. Their carcasses littered the prairie. Matt planned to go out regularly to check on his herd, sweep snow away with pine boughs from the pastures so they could graze, haul out any trapped in drifts, massage ice-congealed eyes so they could see again, break through the frozen pools and river-edges so they could drink, fight off marauding wolves, or rustlers come to that, and generally nurse them through so they could be fattened in the summer and ready for the slaughter yards.

'Looks like it's gonna be another bad winter,' Caleb whinnied, in his trembly, high-octave voice, poking his nose out the door to smell the air.

'Don't say that for Chrissakes.' Matt

went out and returned to the cabin for his own breakfast. He chewed silently on steak and eggs as Mary bustled about preparing the men's food. The memory of what had happened to the ferryman and his wife returned to him persistently like a sickness in the stomach. He was worried about leaving her and the boy alone, but he knew the only thing to do was to go out and chase the killers off. If you gave men like that a yard, as the saying went, they would take a mile. They had to be shown that to venture on his land wouldn't pay.

'Maybe they've moved on,' he muttered to himself. 'Ain't likely to do a thing like that and hang around.'

'What's wrong, Matt?' Mary sat before him on the other side of the table, her blue eyes concerned. 'You've started talking to yourself.'

'Maybe I'm going crazy. This weather don't bode well. We got enough to do without damn outlaws.' He tried to force a grin, but there was a harsh glint in his grey eyes. 'Me an' the boys'll go take a look for 'em.'

Mary reached out and touched his hand. 'You're not thinking of taking the law into your own hands? Surely Luke can handle them? There's not going to be any rough justice, any lynching?'

'If they attack us we'll have to shoot back and shoot to kill. That's the way it has to be out here. We are our own law. If a man steals cows or horses he gits hung high. That's the unwritten law.'

'It's horrible,' she said. 'Why are men so hard out here? Why do they hold life so cheap?'

'There's a lot of shiftless *hombres* drifted west since the war. They've been taught to kill and they've got used to it. They'd rather rob a man than work. I know how you hate killing and violence, Mary, but we have to stand up to them.'

'Yes, but you don't have to do the killing. You're not sheriff now. Leave it to Luke. Promise me, Matt, there won't be any hanging. Promise me, if you catch any of these men you'll take them back to Oglala for a fair trial.'

'Sure,' he said, relieved to hear a hammering on the door. 'I promise. There's Caleb for his grub.'

Mary opened up and handed out canteens of steaming food to the old-timer. 'How you getting on with the new man?'

'Hech! He's a quaint one. Don't say much.'

'Git that down you and be ready to ride,' Matt shouted. He went into the store-room and dug out several cardboard boxes of ammunition. 'Hell knows, we may be needing these,' he muttered. Back in the cabin he checked the Spencer carbine was fully loaded and propped it against the wall. 'Iffen you go outside keep this handy and your eyes peeled — jest in case thet ole grizzly comes nosin' around. Cain't trust a hungry grizzly. You don't have to kill him. A shot over his head should scare him off. Same goes for any other varmints, animal or otherwise.'

Mary shuddered and pulled herself into him. 'All this talk of guns and killing. Sometimes I hate living in this wilderness. Everything so hostile. The wind, the snow, even the people. What's our boy going to grow up like? I want him to be gentle and decent. He's seven and he hasn't even started school.'

Matt looked down at her delicate but determined face beneath its coils of corn-coloured hair. 'Mary, you teach him his letters, and he learns all he needs to know about the ranch from me, about horses — '

'And guns and cows and hanging men. It's not enough, Matt. He needs to mix with other children. I want him to go to a proper school, get a good education.'

'I guess you're right. He won't like it, but we could board him out in Oglala. He could go to school there.'

'Sometimes,' she sighed, 'I wish we

could go back East. There's so much I miss. Music and books and decent society.'

Matt looked glum as he held her. 'I didn't know you felt like that. I guess it's lonesome for a gal like you out here. But I ain't cut out for city life. You know that. An' there's plenty of crime in cities, come to think of it. It ain't jest out here.'

'True. You're a man of the prairie. I made my choice when I married you. How can I be lonesome when I've got you and Jed? Shall I wake him to say goodbye?'

'No, let him sleep. We'll only be away one night, two at the most.'

'Don't worry about the ranch, Matt. We will get through if we pull together. It's not going to be as bad as last winter, I'm sure.'

'Let's pray you're right.'

'I've packed some lunch and there's flour and bacon and stuff to take.' She clung on to his arm and kissed his cheek. 'Matt, promise me, take care.'

'Sure.' He kissed her lips and gave her a wink. 'You keep that bed nice and warm for me.'

★ ★ ★

They rode all morning through the snow, pausing to check and make tally of knots of cattle, following the river, entering valleys overlooked by high purple cliffs and pine-girt slopes. This was the land of the eagle, lynx, bear and mountain lion where a generation before, the Sioux nation had roamed, masters of the land. There was an uncanny silence, pierced only by the shrill cries of birds and wild beasts. It was as if these cliffs were somehow haunted, stark and sinister, the ghosts of the defeated Indians remaining to watch over them.

It was high noon when John Dog Crandal and his crony, Hambone Jones, heard them coming and took cover behind a big rock on the hillside. They watched the tall, lantern-jawed rancher ride past, followed by the lean, savage-faced 'breed and the two punchers. 'Waal, whaddaya know? Sundown Jack's found himself some new friends,' John Dog chuckled. 'I wonder what he's up to?' He peered along the sights of his longarm, taking a bead on Matthews' back.

'We gonna kill 'em?'

'No, I think not. Looks to me like they're leaving the coast clear. Less go see what goodies he's got in his ranch house. Hear tell he's got hisself a purty li'l wife.'

★ ★ ★

The sun was glimmering high in the grey cloud, or as high as it would get that day, when they reached the bend in the river across which was Captain Herbert Newton's spread that cut Matthews' range in half. It occupied a wide loop of the meandering Snake, which snaked around it, becalmed here. It was prime grass which took

49

a tangent for many miles up the valley of Medicine Creek. 'If he cain't fatten his cattle on that nobody can,' Matt said, looking along at the resumption of his own woody, rocky land that he had laid claim to and which stretched a further ten miles.

They forded the icy water and cantered towards Newton's huddle of ranch houses. Folks called him Captain Newton on account of how he still wore his faded caped cavalry coat and campaign hat and, in his cups, would go on about his exploits in the war fighting the Rebs down Arizona way and at Santa Fe at the Battle of Glorietta Pass when they sent the Yankee hordes running back to Texas. He was a ruddy-faced man, his cheeks inflamed by alcohol and living outdoors. He sported a heavy white moustache, and wore his thinning grey hair long, frontier-style, pinning it back with a scarlet Apache headband. As they rode in they could hear the sound of hammer on metal ringing from the wagon repair shop.

'Hi, there, Herb,' Matt shouted through the barn door. 'How's it going?'

In his shirt sleeves and hatless, the Captain looked up, surprised, hanging on to a glowing piece of wheel rim with a pair of tongs as a man beside him hammered at it. 'What's it look like?' he grunted, never the most sociable of men.

'You need a hand to get it on?' Matt asked, and, uninvited, climbed from his horse.

Newton took a break, wiping the sweat from his nose and touching the scarlet rag around his brow as if to make sure it was still in place. 'OK. Roll that wheel over.'

'Nice piece of work.' Matt admired the big back wheel with its shaved and tapered spokes, the 'dishing' of its outsides (that is to say the shaping of it, like a hollowed-out saucer). 'You make this yourself?'

'Dan here did. He's a master

craftsman. He made the whole damn wagon. How'd'ja like my forge, Matthews? I believe in being organized. Self-sufficiency's the word.'

'Must be all that milit'ry trainin',' Caleb chimed in.

'It helps. Come on, man, don't just stand there. Let's get this on.'

Several pairs of hands were better than two. The metal was soon hammered into place, the wagon levered up, and the wheel fixed snugly on its greased axle.

'Whew!' Captain Newton wiped his hands and glanced curiously at the half-breed. 'Who's he?'

'Sundown Jack by name. He's working for me.'

'Thought maybe I'd seen him some place.'

Sundown gave a scoffing shrug. 'Mebbe you have.'

'Where's the rest of your boys, Cap?'

'Out on the range. Guess you men have earned coffee and biscuits.' Newton pulled on his heavy coat, with its tarnished gilt buttons and officer's gold braid, and led them to his ranch house. A girl of about seventeen, dressed like a boy in jeans and check shirt was chopping wood outside.

'Hey, who's the purty gal?' Sundown asked, giving a low whistle. 'She is a gal, ain't she?'

'She's my daughter, Lou, and you can keep your scurvy eyes off her, you no-good dog.'

The men laughed as Sundown Jack clearly had no intention of obeying the command. In fact, he stood close before her, hands on hips, and appraised her. 'Yessir, boss, very nice.'

The slim, dark-haired girl flushed slightly, although it might have been from chopping wood. She gathered an armful and pushed past him, acting cool, pretending to be unruffled by Sundown's attentions. 'Coffee's on the stove. Help yourselves,' she called.

The men clattered into the log house and Sundown went to follow, but Captain Newton placed a hand on his chest. 'You wait outside. I don't allow no Indians nor 'breeds in my home.'

Sundown's face was expressionless as he eyed him, but did as he was told. 'Sure, boss.'

'He's a wild one,' Caleb whooped, warming his hands at the stove. 'You better watch that boy, Cap, or he'll be whisking her away.'

'Nobody whisks me,' the girl said. 'Lou ain't interested in trash like that. You tell him that.'

Matt didn't reply to that, but asked, 'You heard about the Johnson couple?'

'Yes, outrageous. A terrible thing.'

'Would you be interested in getting your boys to ride with us and hound down the scum who did it?'

'Waal, I don't know.' The captain hummed and hahed as he stared at the stove. 'No man is an island and all that kind of thing. But I haven't got time to go riding off on some wild goose chase. They'll be miles away by now.'

'Mebbe. Mebbe not. You ain't seen any of 'em, any drifters hanging around, have you, Herb?'

'No, I've seen nothing, nobody.'

Matt noticed Lou open her lips, as if to say something, but demurred. 'How about you, Lou? You git around quite a bit on that pony of yourn. Seen anybody suspicious-lookin'?'

'No!' she glanced at her father. 'I've seen nobody, neither.'

'You see anybody scurvy-lookin' you better put your spurs to your pony, pronto,' Caleb shouted, 'an' make a beeline back home. Those *hombres* ain't nice to know, missy.'

'She knows how to handle herself,' the captain said. 'She's been ridin' the range since she was twelve, since her mother died. She can ride better and shoot straighter than most men.'

'She sure don't seem fond of wimmin's work,' Elijah guffawed, eyeing the pile of dirty dishes in the sink, the general disarray of the room.

'What's it to do with you?' Lou

snapped, leaning back and watching them.

'You had any rustling?' Matt asked.

'No. Nobody's touched my herd. I guess they wouldn't dare. If they do, I'll willingly ride with you, Matthews. In my opinion we've more to fear from the weather than rustlers.'

'I ain't so sure. From all accounts these are a murderous bunch.'

4

Mary was busy churning butter, patting it into oblong shapes with wooden spatulas and pressing their seal into each half-pound for she planned to sell it next time they visited Oglala. It would help out with expenses. She knew Matt's bank account was extremely low. What cattle they had were in such poor shape after the previous winter it had hardly been worth making the long trail to Cheyenne to sell them. He had decided to overwinter them and try to recoup his fortunes next summer. Since coming to Wyoming she had turned her hand to many tasks she had never imagined a well-brought-up young woman like her would have to do. There was little respite from her tasks, cooking, weaving, fetching wood and water, up at dawn to milk their three milch cows in the barn and milking again in the evening, baking bread and biscuits, washing and darning, even gutting, skinning and curing game, drying fish, making preserves and attending to her stores. She had never dreamed she would learn to shoot a carbine, or would allow her son to be taught how to at his age — of course, it was strictly for taking pot-shots at critters who invaded the henhouse. It was a hard life on the Western frontier and her previous cosseted existence on the East coast seemed like some long-gone dream.

'Where's Pa gone to?' Jed asked, as he sat with his schoolbooks at the table.

'He's gone to check on the herd.'

'What was the sheriff doing here with that little girl?'

'There are some bad men around. Your father has gone to warn them off our land.'

'Will he shoot them?'

'Don't talk like that. Your father will abide by the law.'

'Are you glad he's not a lawman any more?'

Mary bustled about attending to her baking. 'I certainly am. It's far too dangerous a job. Have you finished your sums yet?'

'Not yet,' he murmured, frowning and taking up his crayon. 'Why's Pa digging that big cellar at the back?'

'You know why. To get rid of that old lean-to. A nice big cellar where we can keep our food, sides of smoked bacon, game, butter and cheese. It will be lovely and cool in the summer. And, if there's another hurricane or big twister, we can get down there and be safe.'

The men had already dug the cellar as an extension at the back of the cabin, lined it with flat stones from the river and laid stout pine poles across, notching them together so they would hold firm. Across that they would lay a thick layer of sods. In the big blow of the previous winter families had been frozen to death in their thin-walled shacks, whereas, they had heard, others had survived by huddling out of the blast inside dugouts.

'Your father's looking to the future. One day this is going to be a real big prosperous ranch. He's planning to build me a proper dairy. And a smokehouse so we can cure the hogs when they're slaughtered.'

'I don't like it when they kill the hogs. They squeal so. Why do we have to?'

'Nobody likes it, but, honey, it's them or us. We need to eat meat to stay alive. And we need animal tallow for candles and their skins and furs for clothes. It's a long winter out here. It's the only way to survive.'

'Yes, I suppose so. They don't really understand, do they?'

'They're on a lower rung of the evolutionary tree.'

'What's evolution-ry?'

Mary smiled as she wrapped the

butter in muslin. 'Honey, I'll tell you about that another day. It's a long story.'

'Gee, Ma, you sure know a lot. Where did you learn it all?'

'Well, my father was a professor. I guess I picked it up from him.'

'What, when you were travelling around with him on his lecture tours?'

'Yes. I had to copy his manuscripts for him, take care of his bookings and correspondence, so a lot of what he believed in rubbed off on me.' She smiled again, but this time more wryly as she recalled the months and years spent travelling about America with her father. She had been little more than his unpaid amanuensis, given no freedom under his heavy presence, living under his gloomy shadow. It was true they had a nice house in Boston to which they occasionally returned, but most of their time was spent visiting one obscure town after another until they fused into misty sameness. She had expected to go on in the same way into lonely spinsterhood looking after her widowed father. In some ways, although she did not like to think so, his death had been a blessing for her.

'What happened to Gran'pa?'

'He gave a lecture in Oglala. The hall was packed for the occasion. Halfway through he had a sudden heart attack and fell from the platform. He died in my arms.'

'Why?'

'Because . . . because . . . well, he was quite old. He was a good man, if misunderstood. He was a great believer in Mr Darwin. But we had a lot of trouble because people don't like those views.'

'Why?'

'They think that if we deny the Creation in the Bible — that the world was made in seven days — we deny the existence of God. That is not true. I believe in Darwin, but I thank God every day for his providence. I thank Him for giving me a good husband and a fine son.'

'Why are you crying, Mother?'

'I don't know,' she said, brushing away the tears. 'Because I'm happy, I suppose.'

'How did you meet Pa?'

Mary smiled at the boy again. He had heard the story but she knew he liked to hear it again. 'He was the lawman in Oglala when my father died. He was very kind and took care of things for me. I knew as soon as I looked into his eyes that he was the man I wanted to marry.'

'Why, is he different to other men?'

'Yes, very different. So many men grow up cruel and ignorant and turn into bullies and cowards and drunkards. I thank God every day that your father is sober, industrious and reliable. If you grow up like him I'll be very pleased.'

'Yes, Pa is nice. A bit grumpy at times.'

'That's just his way. He's got a lot to think about.'

'I'm glad he gave up being a lawman. He might have gotten killed.'

'Yes, he well might. Or been forced to kill men. It is demeaning. What is the tenth commandment? 'Thou shalt not kill'. My father was a pacifist. He brought me up to respect life.'

'What's pacifist?'

'Your grandfather refused to fight in the war. They put him in prison. We were shunned socially. Eventually he agreed to serve in the medical corps tending the wounded. The war turned out to be a terrible folly that tore the nation asunder.'

'But if the South attacked us . . . ?'

'You don't understand. Let's see what you've done with these sums.' She sat beside him, made some corrections, and murmured, 'That's good. That's very good. I'm giving you eight out of ten. Next month we might go on to fractions.'

'What are they?'

'You'll find out. I'm going to boil these shirts and underclothes. You can give me a hand to stoke up the fire.'

'Hurrah!' Jed scrambled down and

followed her outside to where they had made a fire under an iron grill on which Mary placed a big pan and filled it with water. She scrubbed on her washboard at the collars and cuffs of the shirts and blouses, and, as the water began to boil and bubble merrily, stood over the pan and poked at the clothes with her pale washing stick.

'We'll leave them to soak a while,' she said. 'We've got to look smart if we're visiting Oglala.'

★ ★ ★

John Dog Crandal set hunched up on his horse in the cover of the pines and watched the cornhaired woman outside the cabin in the valley. She was playing snowballs with her small son, running back and forth, their voices and laughter ringing out in the clear air. The homespun dress was tight about her ample figure and as she bent to scoop up handfuls of snow John Dog

65

gave a low whistle. 'Look at the body on that.'

'Yuh,' Hambone grunted. 'Look at her bosoms bobbin'. We gonna have us some of that?'

'We sure are, boy.' John Dog's eyes narrowed craftily. 'There ain' a soul about. While the mice is away us rats'll play.' He gave a low crackling laugh and spurred his mustang out of the trees and down the slope, followed by Hambone on his piebald. When they reached the valley bottom they pulled in and ambled towards the cabin, nice and easy so as not to frighten her.

They were some hundred paces away, the horses' hooves making little sound on the thin carpeting of snow, when Jed pointed a finger. 'Look, Ma. Men comin'.'

Mary was stooping with her back to them, rolling a handful of snow. She stood and turned, her flushed countenance becoming tense when she saw the dark-bearded man in his ragged frock coat, his burly young sidekick.

'What — who are you?' she called.

John Dog reined in a few paces from her, leaned on his saddle horn, and grinned down at her. 'Jest weary travellers, lady. Can you give us a bite to eat?'

'No. I'm sorry. We have nothing. You had better be on your way.' She could see the lechery smouldering in the gaunt man's dark eyes, see the big revolver stuck in his belt, the Kentucky longarm strapped across his back. Didn't Luke say they had found an old-fashioned ball in the Johnson man's chest? She shuddered, involuntarily, and it was not just from the cold.

'You sayin' you won't give us nuthin' to eat?' Crandal drawled with a sneer. 'That ain't hospitable, lady.'

'No.' Mary backed away a few feet. 'My husband and his men will be back in a short while. They won't take kindly to finding your sort here. You had better be on your way.'

'What's she mean, our sort?' Hambone

yelled. 'Whass she givin' us that lip fer?'

'You better do as my mom says,' Jed piped up from over at the pile of logs where he was standing. 'My dad used to be a lawman.'

'Gee whiz, a lawman! Them's the sort I like.' Hambone jumped down from the piebald and pointed a threatening finger at the boy. 'You better pipe down, pipsqueak, or I'll take pleasure in making you.'

'Jed,' Mary called, sharply. 'Go back in the cabin.'

'Yeah. Maybe you better had, kid. You wouldn't want to watch me pleasurin' your mama.' John Dog swung from the saddle, took off his longarm and laid it aside, stepped towards her. 'She looks like she's wantin' it.'

Mary screamed and tried to fight off the man as he snatched at her. 'You keep your filthy hands — How dare you!'

'Oh, I dare.' Crandal's foul breath

was in her face as he pulled her to him, tried to kiss her. 'Jones, keep an eye on that brat while I git a hold on this wild cat.'

Hambone drew his Colt and covered the boy. 'You jest don't do nuthin', sonny, if you wanna live.'

Jed stared at him, wide-eyed with fear, stared across at the other man, at what he was doing to his mother.

'You damn bitch,' Crandal hissed, as Mary scratched at his face and kicked. He back-handed her across the jaw, grabbed hold of her dress front, and ripped it and her bodice apart. 'Hey, look at them beauties,' he gloated, as her milk-white, deep-cleft breasts tumbled out.

Hambone turned to watch, his lips slavering. John Dog swiftly put a boot behind Mary's legs and threw her to the ground. 'Hurry it up,' Hambone shouted, as Crandal stood over her, fumbling at his clothes. 'I want my turn.'

Her lips trickling blood, her head

ringing from the blow, Mary lay in the mud and snow and watched, with horror, the tall man uncovering himself. A panic rose in her throat: she knew he would kill her, kill her son. She scrambled away as the men laughed, rolled to her feet, and ran towards the fire. Crandal chased after her. 'No, you don't, sister.'

Mary reached for the big pan of boiling water, picked it up by its handles, turned to face him, and hurled the water and soggy washing over him.

Crandal screamed as the scalding water hit him full-face. He put his hands to his eyes, and flailed about, blinded, but trying to catch hold of her. Mary dodged out of his way, reached around his waist and whipped his revolver from his belt.

'Hey, you!' Hambone shouted, strutting towards her, his revolver-hand outstretched. 'What are you doin'? Drop that.'

Mary stood, the revolver half-raised, as Crandal staggered about and cursed.

She looked into the eyehole of the younger man's Colt and, in a half-daze, slowly tossed the revolver away, resigning herself to her fate.

Hambone Jones grinned at her and started forward. 'Thass better. You learnin' some sense. What he started, I'm gonna finish, lady.'

His close-cropped, ugly, leering face, was almost upon her, when he juddered and twisted, his mouth and eyes an agony of pain. A shot had hammered out and into his back. 'Uh?' he grunted, and fell forward into the snow by her feet.

'You leave my mom alone,' Jed's voice was trembling. 'Or I'll shoot you again. And you, mister. Get outa here.'

The boy, in his homespun suit and muffler, was standing holding the smoking Spencer carbine, jerking the lever to slide another bullet into the breech. The carbine had been left leaning against the cabin wall but had toppled over to lie concealed

71

behind the logpile. That's where Jed had found it.

'What'n hell's happening?' John Dog croaked, blinking his eyes, his face red raw from the blistering water.

'Jed!' Mary screamed. 'Don't! Put that down.'

'They was going to do things to you, Mom.'

Mary stared at the broad back of the fallen youth which was beginning to curdle blood through the coat. 'I think you've killed him,' she whispered.

She picked up Crandal's longarm as he made a move towards her, jabbed it into his chest. 'Get back. Get out of here. We see you again we'll kill you, too.'

John Dog peered at her, seeing again, if hazily, and whimpered as he touched his face. 'I'm goin'.'

He found his horse and climbed into the saddle. 'I'm going,' he shouted. 'But I'll be back for you. I'll burn you down.'

Jed ran to his mother and she hugged

him to her as they watched the man in his ragged coat go riding away towards the hills. 'Maybe we should've taken him into the sheriff, Ma? Maybe we shouldn't have let him go?'

'Oh, my God!' She gave a sigh of despair as she stared at the dead young man. 'What have we done?'

'It was them or us, Ma.'

'Was it? Come on inside.' She pulled her dress together to cover herself, led him back indoors.

'If only your father were here,' she said, as she slammed the shutters, bolted the door, sat at the table, tried to calm herself.

'I don't think that man will come back now.'

'No, I don't think he will.' But she knew his sort never gave up. It was going to be a long night, waiting and listening in case he did return. 'This dreadful country,' she groaned, staring at her son. 'Seven years old and a killer!' She felt the tears rolling down her cheeks, the shudders of delayed shock. 'I don't think I can stand it much longer.'

'Come on, Ma,' Jed said, awkwardly, tenderly touching her. 'Pa will know what to do. He will say we did right. Won't he?'

5

Sundown Jack whirled his little mustang, Smoke, looking about him at slopes, scarred and pine-stubbled, the snow shadowed by the fast-lowering sun. He sniffed at the air, like a questing animal, both forward and back the way they had come.

'What's the matter?' Matthews asked him.

'I don't know. I got a feeling down my back. Something wrong. Something bad happen.'

'Where?'

Sundown shrugged. 'It over. We too late, anyhow. We find out pretty soon.'

Matt looked uneasily at the other two riders.

'We'll press on,' he said. 'Johnson's ferry ain't far ahead.'

There were no wagon roads where they were going, only pony or deer trails between the pastures that bordered the Snake River. Where the high canyon sides closed in the water would tumble and churn through short abrupt rapids. And then seem to slow as it flowed on into gleaming flat pools. It was beside one of these they found the snow and mud churned and reddened by blood.

'Look at that!' Caleb shouted, pointing to a frozen carcass. 'She's been slow-elked. Left for the wolves.'

'I got eyes,' Matt muttered, his face grim.

But worse was to come. As they followed the river's bends they came across more killing grounds. Evidence of wholesale slaughter was scattered across the ground. Horned heads, hooves, innards and other offal left in a foul mess.

Matt sat his horse and tried to swallow his disgust, nearly choking on the words. 'They couldn't be content with the steers. They had to take my best breeding cows and calves.'

Elijah picked up a piece of discarded

hide. 'It's your brand, sure enough, Mistuh Matthews.'

'Yeah,' Matt grunted, trying to make a mental count of how many they had taken, how much it would cost them. Thousands of dollars, that was to be sure.

'Lookee here,' Caleb cried. 'There's wagon tracks. Purty heavy load.'

'It would be.'

'Thass goin' slow 'em down,' Sundown Jack hissed. 'They can only be day ahead.'

'Yes,' Matt thundered. 'There's going to be a reckoning for this.'

The tracks led to the Johnsons' cabin, the flatbottom ferry pulled up on the bank. Matt took a look inside, picked up an empty jug. 'Looks like they had a party.'

It was an eerie, desolate place in the twilight, and he shivered and climbed back on his horse. 'We'll press on to the line cabin,' he said. 'We cain't go much further tonight.'

As they rode on he asked Jack, 'This

the way your friends usually operate?'

'Nope.' The 'breed's face was solemn as he glanced at the rancher. 'I guess they wanted to get rid of the brands.'

'Where you reckon they're heading?'

He shrugged and grimaced. 'Maybe along the Snake. The country up ahead's riddled with ravines they could hide out in. Maybe down the Little Snake towards Troublesome. Trail easy enough to follow if we don't git another fall.'

They both looked, apprehensively, at the sky. It was a clear, still night, a pale globe of moon beginning to climb up from behind the crags into its nightly arc. The first stars had begun to glitter. But a squall could blow up from nowhere.

'The hosses are too tuckered out to go any further tonight,' Matt said, as they reached Dead Man's ravine. 'The cabin ain't far now.'

They climbed up through the brush in the half-darkness until old Caleb's leading horse whinnied and shied and the 'puncher wheezed out, 'There's somethin' lyin' in the snow. It's a big elk.'

'An elk?' Matt echoed, mystified. 'It's been shot?'

'No.' Caleb jumped down to peer at it from beneath his big Stetson. 'Look at the tines on them antlers. It's a big ole buck elk. Something's dragged it down, made a mess of its head. It ain't wolves. Something with real sharp claws. It ain't bear.'

'Wolverine.' Sundown Jack was examining padmarks in the snow. There was something akin to fear in the whites of his eyes as he looked around at the dark, brooding trees. 'His claws and teeth are like razors. It's the only critter the bear's feared of.'

'Wolverine?' Matt had heard of this beast but never seen one. He knew from descriptions that the furry, short-tailed creature was short and squat, not more than three feet in length and the largest member of the weasel family. 'If he can do this to an elk what's he gonna do to my cattle? What few I got left.'

'The Sioux call him the Evil One,' Jack whispered, huskily. 'He's got so much frenzied power he can kill critters many times his size. Sometimes he jest kills for blood lust. He's bad news, boss.'

'He sure is. Bad news is all we're gettin' today.'

'What we gonna do?' Elijah asked.

'We're all saddle-weary. We come a long way. This is fresh meat. We'll carve off a haunch, go git some grub inside us.'

Sundown Jack peered into the forest. 'Mebbe he's still around? Mebbe we jest sceered him off.'

★ ★ ★

The little cabin beneath the snowy pines in the dusk of Dead Man's Creek was a welcome sight. They soon had the horses fed and hobbled and pine knots roaring in the tin stove. There

80

was not a lot of room for four grown men, but the cabin was double-bunked on either side so it soon became cosily warm. That was if a man didn't mind Elijah's sweaty socks swinging about his nose, for Matt had claimed the bottom bunk and Elijah was on top. Nothing, however, could spoil the gorgeous scent of elk steak and wild onions that spluttered in the pan. When they had eaten they lay back and rested their saddle-sore limbs.

Sundown Jack's wide nostrils twitched fastidiously. It was plain to see he was not fond of being in close contact with smelly and sweaty white men. He reached for his carbine and drawled, 'I think I go take a look further along the river. Moon's high. Maybe I can see something of them *hombres*.'

'You ain't thinkin' of runnin' off with 'em agin?' Caleb chuckled.

'I tell you. Me and them, we're through. I tell you something else, the man who lead them, he's as mean and ornery as that wolverine. They should call *him* Evil One.'

He gave them a baleful look and slipped out, and they heard him muttering to his bronc as he saddled him, and the muffled sound of hooves as he rode off.

'That Smoke must be tough as nails,' Elijah said.

'Same as his owner,' Matt agreed.

Left on their own, like always, the conversation turned to the big blizzard of January '86, earlier that year. They recalled with awe the strange yellowing purple that had bordered the northern horizon on the first day of the year. How a drizzle had begun, the temperature dropping rapidly, the rain turning into razor-sharp hail swept by a hurricane from the north. That night the range country from the Dakotas down through to Kansas and even further south on into Texas was lashed by the greatest white-out in known history.

All landmarks and trails were obliterated as it raged across the land.

Matt and his family had piled logs on the fire and shivered as the cabin shook. The hope was the blizzard would soon pass. But there was no abatement the second day and by the following night the situation was alarming. Not once did the terrifying wind diminish. It blotted everthing out with a curtain of driving snow. And the cattle? They were swept along before it until they could go no further and fell dead in their tracks. It was not until the thaw and the spring round-up that men saw the extent of the damage: whole herds wiped out.

And the cattle were not the only ones to suffer. Hundreds of cowboys and horses, families taking shelter in flimsy cabins, were found frozen to death. The country further east, Kansas down to the River Arkansas suffered worst, and the big cattle companies: many were bankrupt overnight.

'Doc Barton of the OS Bar spread had twelve thousand head under his brand,' Caleb said. 'He lost them all.

And another lost five thousand at a cost of a hundred thousand dollars. One British outfit jest packed up and went home.'

'Mebbe it'll be our turn this winter,' Elijah muttered, as he swung his feet, encased in the odiferous, holey socks.

'Come on, fellas,' Matt said. 'What you trying to do — give me bad dreams?'

He pondered the situation gloomily. The summer had been dry, with little water and correspondingly poor grass in Wyoming so, what cattle he had were, by the autumn, thin and in poor condition. Now this heavy snow had fallen, blocking some of the higher passes and freezing the streams. Soon it would be Christmas, but that only meant the worst of the five months of winter had yet to begin.

Matt knocked out his pipe, got to his feet and pulled on his bearskin and hat. He picked up his carbine, clacked a slug into the breech and said, 'I'm going out to look for that wolverine.'

The moon had risen high, casting a silvery glow over the scene. He set off riding back along Dead Man's Creek until he reached the brow where they had found the dead elk. Maybe he should follow the tracks, try to find its lair? No, maybe better to wait. The Evil One might return to the scene of the crime for another feed? He hunkered down in the trees, downwind some forty feet. He might well have a long, fruitless wait.

As he squatted there in the moonlight he pondered on life's inequities. He had thought he was doing well, a place of his own all paid for, a woman and child who had brought him great bliss. After all the fighting and living dangerously as a lawman he thought he might have found a bit of peace at last. As he listened to the wind whining through the trees he knew that Nature was not through. Maybe he was wasting his time? Another succession of blizzards and his cattle would never survive in their weakened state. He knew that. And now these killers on the prowl. Another problem to taunt and haunt him. Whoever killed the Johnsons, should be called the Evil Ones. Suddenly he knew he should never have left Mary and the boy alone.

And, as suddenly, there was a spitting snarl and he saw yellow eyes flickering in the moonlight, almost upon him, the creature running fast towards him from an oblique angle, its fangs bared and, as he raised the carbine, it was leaping upon him, bowling him over, its claws tearing at his throat.

6

Sundown Jack could smell them half a mile away before he found them, the white man's unwashed sweat, the raw whiskey, the blood of the carcasses, as did his pinto, Smoke, who whinnied his disgust. Jack cantered the pony carefully along the icy bank of the southern confluent, the Little Snake, and saw their fire a short way on from the river's fork. He slipped from the saddle and loosehitched his bronc to a bough, treading forward silently on foot until he could see the silhouettes of four figures huddled in their soogans around the fire. He thumbed back the hammer of his revolver and peered under the canvas flap into the wagon. It was piled high with raw meat. Beef was scarce since last winter's blizzard and it would be worth a good price in Troublesome.

Sleeping like babes, he thought, as he listened to the men's resonant snores. I could cut all their throats and take this little lot back. But he was not a man who cared to kill by stealth, or kill at all without call. And he wasn't sure yet that this was any of his business. He had only agreed to ride with Matthews because it was better than being strung up by the posse.

They had brought the dead ferryman's mule along and it must have scented his mustang for it suddenly gave a hoarse, hawing bray, and one of the men stirred, raising himself on an elbow. Jack recognized the cunning, slit-eyed face of El Cuchillo, the Knife Man.

'Howdy, Estevez.' He gave a grin as he pointed the old Frontier revolver at the Mexican's heart and watched his hand slide towards the throwing blade stuck in the ground near his head. 'I wouldn't if I was you. This might go off. Where's John Dog?'

'He no here. He gone maraudin''

back toward that ranch.'

'That so? Who with?'

'Hambone. What to you? What you want here?'

The other men began to stir, Seedy Smith, looking like a scarecrow in his ragged suit, straw hair hanging from his battered hat. 'Sundown Jack!' He, too, began to reach for his rifle, but Jack waggled the big Colt Frontier, indicating him not to. 'What you doin' back?'

'Thass what I ask heem,' the Mexican hissed.

Snake Eyes Finnegan had woken up and was scratching at his ginger thatch. 'Can't a man be gettin' any sleep?'

'What's goin' on?' Slippery Williams called from across the fire, fumbling for the gun in his greatcoat pocket but changing his mind when he saw the 'breed with the Frontier. 'Waal, if it ain' ole Jack. You decided to rejine us?'

'I ain't decided nuthin' yet,' Jack said. 'Boys, I did'n like what you done to that ferryman and his missis. Thass why I took a few pots at you and lit out with the kid. But I was one of you once an' I ain' inclined to turn you in.'

'You ain'?' Estevez drawled. 'That mighty good of you.'

'It is, 'cause I coulda killed you all jest now had I a mind to. You got a good haul of beef. I suggest you move on along with it and don't come back this way no more.'

'You do, huh?' Slippery propped himself up against his saddle and rolled a cigarette. 'That ain' up to me, 'breed. That's up to John Dog.'

'An' I'm tellin' you to move on out.' Jack's eyes gleamed dark and deadly in the firelight. 'You can give the same message to John Dog.'

'Whass the matter with you?' Seedy hooted. 'Why you turned all Holy Joe all a sudden? Why you turned against your mates?'

'My boots would be kickin' air if it weren't for that rancher, Matthews. I owe him. So, I'm warnin' you an' you tell John Dog Crandal. Take what you've got an' go. Otherwise you all an' me gonna have a fallin' out.'

'Come on, Jack, me auld lad,' Finnegan said. 'No need to be like that. Why this change of heart?'

'You're not so bad,' Jack said. 'I got nuthin' 'gainst a spot of rustlin', same as you. But when it comes to rapin' and killin' of wimmin, I'm out.'

'Aw, the boys was all whiskied up. That won't happen again. You an' me won't let it. We'll keep a rein on Crandal. Come on, Jack, we'll make a tidy sum on this cargo. You're a rustler at heart. We need a wild boyo like you.'

Estevez laughed. 'Maybe John Dog already done some more rapin' and killin'. He say he go back to take look at that rancher's wife.'

'He did?' Sundown Jack's face froze and a chill seemed to run up his spine. He glanced back to the direction he had come, at the Little Snake river bubbling on its way from the fork.

'You tell John Dog if he hurt that woman I will come after him. I will send him to Hell where he belongs.'

He backed away keeping his eyes on them and slipped into the darkness of the pines. 'Yeah, clear off,' he heard Seedy howl. 'You think John Dog's scared of you, you lousy 'breed? He don't give a damn. None of us do.'

Sundown gritted his teeth together as he headed back to his horse, an anger surging in him. Maybe it would have been better if he had killed them all, got it done with?

* * *

Matt Matthews groaned as he regained consciousness, surprised to see the icy crags towering over him, etched against the starry sky. Something, someone was shaking at him, shaking him back out of the sleep of death, the cold sleep from which no man returns.

Memory returned to him, vividly: the snarling fangs tearing into him, the wild creature, the wolverine, biting and clawing at him, his face, his throat, his legs, like something demented, as he was tumbled back into the snow, kicking out at it, trying to aim the carbine, the explosion as he fired, and knowing he had missed. But the sound scared the critter off and he saw it go bounding away across the snowy hillside, turning once to gaze at him malevolently. He had lain there, his blood pumping out of him, and he had tried to tie his bandanna tight around his throat to staunch the flow. There was a searing pain in his leg, but he got to his feet and, leaning on the carbine for support began to head back towards the cabin.

That short journey of half a mile was one of the longest of his life. He kept collapsing, rolling down the hillside, and had lain, staring up at the icy stars revolving about him, and had forced himself to get up, stagger on, not knowing if he was going the right way, a panic in him, of the Dark

Avenger hovering over him, of the Evil One returning to attack him again. He reached the ice-covered stream, Dead Man's Creek, and suddenly remembered he had a horse, and had left her behind tied to a pine. He had wanted to go back but, in a moment of clarity, he knew his only chance was to go on. Oddly enough, the legend of Hugh Glass had returned to him, the famed frontiersman, who, severely mauled by a grizzly bear, had been abandoned by his party, but had crawled on his hands and knees 200 miles back to Fort Kiowa through this very same country. What was his struggle compared to that? By that time Matt had lost his carbine and was crawling through the snow, too. There was the cabin in the silent glade of firs. But he was not sure he could make it. He clawed with supplicating hands, tried to pull himself on, croaked out a cry of anger and pain as the darkness closed over him. His last desperate thought, as bitter as the taste of blood in his mouth, was that he had failed his wife, his son, even his poor horse.

'Come on, ye're not gone yet,' a voice said, strong arms pulling him up out of the snow. 'Here, put an arm over me shoulder. We need to git ye in the warm.'

The half-frozen-to-death rancher, weak from loss of blood, did as he was bid and hung onto the man in his rough jacket and fringed buckskins, the man he hazily recognized as Sundown Jack. 'You were right about that critter,' he croaked out. 'He went berserk.'

Jack staggered under his weight towards the small cabin. 'What them other lazy bastards up to — fast asleep, I have no doubt,' he grunted, kicking open the door.

Caleb jumped up, bumping his head against the top bunk. 'What in hail?'

'Git that stove fired up,' Sundown said. 'The boss he blue with cold. Put some big stones on top.'

'Jeez?' Elijah peered down from his

bunk with awe as Matt was laid down. 'What happened?'

'What do you think? That wolverine near tore off his head. Look at this bite in his neck. Just missed the jugular. He lost lot of blood but he lucky to be 'live.'

'Whoo, he sure is. That critter's teeth cut clean through his leather chaps. Looks like his bearskin coat saved him from gittin' his chest tore apart.'

'Maybe the Evil One think him a bear. They enemy, you know. We better heat up some stones.'

Caleb started tossing pine knots into the tin stove. 'What you want stones for?'

'Wrap 'em in shirts. We got to warm him. We got to git his body heat back. You OK, boss?'

Matt nodded, his blue lips unable to form words.

'I pack snow on the neck wound. It better than hot water. You lie still. We gonna git you back home.'

'I'll brew up some coffee. Git

something warm inside him.'

Sundown studied the gaping wound in the neck, still oozing blood. 'Why you men not go look for him when he don't come back?'

'Aw,' Caleb whined. 'I like my shut-eye. I ain't one for moseyin' around in the dark. Mist' Matthews kin gen'rally look after himself.'

'Not against the Evil One he cain't. You gotta look after the boss or you'll be outa job.'

* * *

John Dog Crandal hauled in his horse, harshly, when he saw through his enflamed eyes the signs of struggle in the snow. 'What's been goin' on here?' he asked. The full moon was high and casting a silvery glow over the forest and, by its light, he followed the bloodstained trail. It was like the wavering footsteps of a drunken man, or a badly injured one. He had fallen down and crawled on. 'Just what I need,' Crandal muttered, as he found an abandoned carbine. He jumped down and clacked a bullet into the breech. The trial led on up the creek and he could see the glimmer of light from a cabin. Gingerly, he touched his blistered face. The rage of pain and anger in him made him want to ride up there and finish off whoever was up there. But he did not know how many there might be. Caution bade him stay.

'I'll go git the boys.' His reddened eyes glowed with rage as he stared up the creek and he vowed his vengeance. 'I'll git even. I'll git even with all of 'em. They'll wish they never crossed me.'

John Dog climbed on a terrified mare he found tethered in the trees. He ground his spurs into her sides and charged on along the Snake, leading his own horse. 'I'll be back,' he shouted. 'That man an' his bitch ain't seen the last of me.'

7

'God in heaven,' Matt gasped out as they hauled him on a travois of lodgepoles into the ranch and he saw the frosted corpse of Hambone Jones, sprawled face down where he had been shot. 'What's been going on?'

Mary's heart skipped a beat when she saw her husband's pallor, the bloodstained rag around his throat. 'Oh, my God,' she cried. 'What's happened?'

'What's happened to you, Mary?' Matt croaked out, huskily.

'Don't you worry about me. We must see to you first. Don't try to move. We'll carry you into the house.'

She directed them to lie him on their bed of bearskins, as Jed watched, wide-eyed. She carefully unwrapped the sticky bandage and winced when she saw the width of the cut. 'Put a pan of water on. I'm going to have to put stitches in this or he'll bleed to death.'

Mary took a deep breath, tried to steady her nerves, then went to find her big sewing needle, the length of gut she sometimes used to make jackets of leather. 'This is going to have to do,' she said, placing the needle in the pan to sterilize it. 'It's no use sending for that drunken Doc Bowdrey in Oglala. There's no time.'

Caleb put a wooden spatula between Matt's teeth and held him as she carefully sewed the wound together with seven stitches, snipping each neatly as she had seen in an illustrated medical book. She sighed with relief when it was done and put on a clean dressing.

Matt's grey eyes met her blue ones. 'What happened here, Mary?'

'It was them or us. They would have killed us.'

'I did it, Pa,' Jed blurted out. 'They were hurtin' Mom. I shot him. He's dead. I didn't mean to kill him. Will they hang me, Pa?'

'Of course they won't.' Mary pulled the boy into her, tears streaming down her face. 'You did right. Tell him he did right, Matt.'

Matt studied them, solemnly for seconds, remembering his wife's hatred of killing. 'Yes, you did right, son.'

'Sure you did,' Caleb said. 'You gotta protect your ma. Everybody knows that. They'll give you a reward. Thass what they'll do. I bet there's a ree-ward on that bad-ass's head.'

'Please, Caleb,' Mary turned to him. 'Don't talk like that.'

'You'll have to go in see Luke Hanlon, Mary, explain,' Matt whispered, huskily. 'Git Sundown Jack to take you. He's a good man.'

'Of course. You sleep now, Matt. You've got to rest, get your strength back.'

'Yeah, I'm gonna need my strength if I'm gonna catch up with that bunch.'

'You gotta take it easy, boss,' Caleb

wheezed. 'You sure ain' gonna be doin' any ridin' and fightin' for a while.'

★ ★ ★

The day dawned icily chill but cloud free. Sundown Jack had the buggy ready for an early start. He kicked at the corpse on the ground. It was frozen solid. He had to hack with an axe to release Hambone Jones's boots from the ground. He looped a rawhide rope around his ankles and tied it to the back of the rig. Mary came from the cabin with Jed, both mother and son looking pale but determined. She had a black woollen scarf tied around her head and wound around her throat, and was wearing a red cape trimmed with beaver fur.

'Matt seems to be resting better. He thinks we ought to both go in to answer any questions.' Caleb helped her up to sit beside Jack on the front seat of the buggy and Jed climbed up alongside.

102

'You wrap that blanket round your legs and chest,' she said. 'We don't want you catching cold. How about you, Jack? Do you want to borrow a topcoat of Matt's?'

'No, missis. I'se OK.' Sundown had only the worn old suit-jacket over his red wool shirt, a bandanna around his throat. He seemed impervious to the icy wind. He pulled his high-crowned black hat down over his brow and whacked at the buggy-horse with a lariat end. 'Less go!'

The horse pawed and strained and the body of Hambone gave a crack and came away from its resting place, trailing along like a toboggan as the rig went bobbing away. They had a long ride across the prairie and they didn't speak much all the way. Indeed, it was too cold to open the mouth for long. By noon they sighted the tumbledown town of false fronts along a wide main street. Folks stopped and stared at them as they wheeled in, the corpse sliding along behind.

'There'll have to be an inquest,' Luke Hanlon said, as he hauled the 'stiff' unceremoniously into his office. 'When he's thawed out I'll git the doc to take a look at him.'

'Jed's very upset. Does he have to be involved?'

'I'm afraid he does, Mary. The coroner will want to hear how he come to shoot him. We'll try to go easy on the boy.'

Oglala didn't have a lot to offer, but it had an eatery and they hurried into this for some warm soup. The people at the other tables eyed them curiously, the haughty blonde-haired woman, her boy, and the dark, sour-looking 'breed with his black, shoulder-length hair and beaded headband.

When they had eaten Mary looked at Sundown frankly and said, 'I think I have you to thank for saving my husband's life.'

Sundown grinned and shrugged as he saw some rubber-neckers staring rudely at them through the window of the restaurant. 'I jest did what I could,' he said.

'Folks don't have much manners in these parts,' Mary replied, frowning at the onlookers as she sipped her coffee.

'Guess they think it kinda funny, you invitin' me in here like this.'

'Why so?'

He shrugged again, a flicker of warmth lurking in his dark eyes. 'I like you, missis. You got good grit. Your man's a lucky guy. So's your boy.'

Mary reached out a pale hand and touched him. 'Thank you, Jack.' She was not sure why but she found herself blushing. 'Will you stay on at the ranch?'

'I ain' one to stay long nowhere, Mary.' He smiled crookedly, as she removed her hand. 'But I guess I'll bide a while.'

'I don't know. I might be going back East. I don't think I can stand it out here any longer. I haven't told Matt yet. I wish you would stay on and help him out. Would you do that, Jack?'

He was silent for a while, brooding on this. 'If you stayed I would sure help you.'

Mary met his eyes and flushed again. 'It's nearly time for the inquest to start. We had better go.'

★ ★ ★

The coroner mopped his dripping nose and took a none-too-discreet pull at a whiskey flask as he listened to the evidence. 'You sound like you was put through quite an ordeal, young lady. We better hear what your boy's got to say.'

'Is that necessary?' Mary asked. 'He's only a child.'

'Yup, lady, I'm 'fraid so. We gotta hear all the evidence. Now, boy, you know what it means to swear on the Bible to tell the truth?'

'Yessir,' Jed said, as he stood up

before all the people crowding the courtroom. 'I didn't mean to kill him. He was goin' to hurt my ma. It was the only way to stop him. I jest pointed the rifle and fired. I didn't think he would die.'

'That sometimes happens, young man, when you fire guns. Let's go through this carefully . . . '

It was an ordeal hearing it all spelled out and written down, but eventually the coroner mopped his face, took another slug, banged his gavel, and announced, 'Verdict, accidental death. And, if I may say so, one richly deserved by the deceased scoundrel. In fact, I'd like to congratulate young Jed on defending his mother so spunkily from such rapacious bandits. The sooner more scum like these are put down the better it will be.'

Mary put her arm around her boy and pushed through the jostling noisy crowd who were trying to pat him on the back. Outside she turned to Sundown and said, 'I think we'll stay the night at the hotel. It's too late to get back now.'

'Sure,' Jack drawled. 'You glad about the verdict? I am. I'll be over the saloon you need me.'

8

Troublesome was a town that had long lived up to its name. It had become the hang-out of drifters, out-of-work cowboys looking for an easy dollar, and various gentlemen of the prairie, whose goings and comings it was not wise to query. The bullet-studded boards of the several saloons testified to arguments that flared up and were easily settled — with six-guns.

John Dog Crandal and his boys rode in on their mustangs alongside the heavily loaded wagon, Slippery Williams on the box cracking a bullwhip over the backs of the draught horses, given extra pulling power by the mule hooked by makeshift harness up front. The few honest farmers who were going about their business at the stores and farrier's gave them a look but decided it was none of their business. The wagon rolled up to Murphy's Meat Mart and creaked to a halt in the mud of the main street.

Murphy, whose close-shaven face was bloodred, and his neck as fleshy as any prize pig's, assessed the consignment, tipped his bowler hat over his nose and scratched the back of his head. 'Where would you have come by this little lot?'

'I bought 'em off a rancher up north a'ways,' Crandal said. 'Saved him the bother of herding 'em to market.'

'Sure, of course it would.' Murphy took a pencil from behind his ear and a notebook from the pocket of his suit that was almost bursting its buttons. He made a few calculations. 'Would you be having a receipt of purchase?'

'Sure I've got a receipt.' Crandal looked at his men and laughed like a hyaena. He produced a dirty scrap of paper. 'Don't think we're dishonest, do ya?'

Murphy studied the receipt, frowning. 'What's dis? A Mister Jones of the

Bar X6. I can't say I've ever heard of him. That's who you bought dis from?'

'A small spread. He ain't been in business long.'

'No, I'm sure he ain't. And no doubt by now he'll have packed up and gone. And your name is Smith?'

'That's me. Jones and Smith. Anything funny about that?'

'No, no, very common names. Far be it from me to suggest they was aliases. Your first name would be John, I've no doubt.'

'How did you know that?'

Murphy shrugged. 'Let's get this stuff off the street. I'll give you fourteen hundred dollars.'

'This beef's worth eighteen hundred,' Crandal growled.

'Not to me it ain't.'

'Look, Murphy, I got my men to pay. They won't be happy if they don't get a decent cut for hauling it in. Will you boys?'

Snake Eyes Finnegan sat his horse

and gave a gappy grin from beneath his old army forage cap. 'We most certainly won't. You know, Mister Murphy, I know some men who might get so upset if they didn't get a decent price they'd come back in the middle of the night and burn this meat mart down. Not that we'd do that, eh, boys?'

'Shucks, no,' Slippery called from his seat on the box. 'Not us. Mind you, I did hear this greaser here' — he jerked a thumb at Estevez — 'is some kinda pyromaniac. Ain't that the word?'

El Cuchillo flicked a match on his nail and lit a cheroot, grinning evilly. 'Wha' that you say?'

'OK, eighteen hundred cash,' Murphy hurriedly agreed. 'I don't know you and you don't know me.'

'Done,' Crandal said. 'Would you be interested in us bringing any more in on the hoof? There's others where these come from.'

'Come over to the office.' Murphy got a clerk to fetch him the cash from his safe and passed it across. 'If you get any more you try to be more discreet, Mister Jones. Or was it Smith?'

'Er, I fergit.'

'We got a law in this town. Abe Ferguson. Big lazy sonuvabitch. Sheriff's wage ain't much so if he gets a little bonus he's not unwilling to look the other way, but we can't be flouting the law openly. There's been a lot of talk in the journals about rustling on the Wyoming range, not that you'd do that.'

'Sure we wouldn't, Mister Murphy.' Crandal flicked through the dollars and tucked 1,000 into his shirt pocket. Two hundred to each of his men ought to satisfy them. 'The very thought.'

'So, if you do purchase any more cattle it might be advisable to keep 'em hid out in the hills and I'll come and take a look at them for ye. Then we'll bring 'em into town under cover of darkness. Just so folks don't get nosy.'

'Suits me,' Crandal said. 'A pleasure to do business with you. Nobody wants to put his head in a noose for no reason, do they?'

★ ★ ★

On stage at the Ace-in-the-Hole a girl was singing:

'Rosie, my sweetest posy,
Come out into the moonlight,
Come out with me,
Rosie, my blessed posy,
I long to kiss you, so blissfully . . . '

The skimpily clad prairie nymph was kicking up her pink-stockinged knees, showing her garters and her frills and furbelows and squawking out the popular ballad, breathlessly, as a quartet of her primped and painted sisters-in-sin pranced about in chorus beside her.

A piano-player rattled the ivories and a pack of lusty, steamed-up men roared their approval, peering up at the flailing limbs on the creaking stage. The singer,

114

in a plaited wig of white string, gave a mischievous wink and poked out her tongue lewdly, as the encore ended, and the curtains were closed. The act was by way of an advertisement of the wares to be found upstairs.

'Yee-hoo!' Seedy Smith shrilled. 'I gonna git myself a basinful of that li'l plump one on the end. You see her makin' eyes at me?'

Why any young woman should want such a scrawny, tattered and pungently unbathed specimen as himself did not occur to him. But no doubt the doxy had noticed him splashing his cash very liberally at the bar.

'Yes, suh!' Slippery grinned, clapping his shoulders. 'Git up them stairs. I'll jine you. I fancy a taste of that singer lady. You s'pose her name really is Rosie?'

They staggered up the rickety stairs to the landing, with Slippery warbling, 'Rosie, my li'l posy . . . '

In a corner of the crowded Ace-in-the-Hole gaming house John Dog

Crandal and Emanuel Estevez were sitting, their backs to the wall, involved in a poker game. A gambling man, his long hair slicked back from his midnight-pallor-sharp features, perfumed, and attired in a silverfaced, pearl-grey frock coat, frilled shirt and goldthreaded vest, smiled, oilily. He had been letting them win as a sweetener.

'I'm ready to raise my bet,' he said. 'How about you gen'lemen?'

'Sure, I came loaded for bear not chickens. I'll throw three hundred US dollars in the pot,' Crandal told him. 'You gonna call me?'

The gambler looked over at a big man called Little Joe who was riding shotgun over the faro, roulette and poker tables — sitting on a highlegged chair with a twelve gauge sawn-off. Joe gave a flicker of a nod. He didn't like the look of these two *hombres* but he reckoned he could handle them.

The owner of the joint, Slim Soames, was leaning against the bar watching the game. He was a lanky man, also stylishly besuited, with a high polish to his blood-red boots. He touched the side of his nose, a signal to the gambler to go for it, and lowered his head to say something to the shirtsleeved barkeep. The balding liquor-operator looked across at the group, and nodded to Soames.

Other men around the table threw in their hand as the stakes were raised too high for them and the game went on. Gradually the pot was swollen. Crandal was on a winning streak. He couldn't lose, he was certain of that. He threw another ill-gotten $200 into the game, greedily. 'I'm ready to bet on this hand,' he snarled. 'You gonna meet me?'

'Sure,' the gambler drawled and with his soft, beringed fingers pushed in another $200 in gold coin. 'I ain't here for a lot of sweet talk and lah-di-dah. I'm here to play poker.'

Crandal hesitated, the unhealed blisters on his cheeks and forehead seeming to turn redder with the tension. There was more than $3,000 in the pot by now. He was certain he had a winning hand. There was no way this effeminate riverboat man could beat him.

'Let's go for it,' he hissed and revealed his cards.

The gambler smiled and showed three aces and the knave of hearts. 'You lose, stranger.' He reached over to draw the pot in. 'That's the luck of the table.'

'Luck of the table,' Crandal spat out. 'You jest hold it right there. Where you git that third ace from? Who you think you dealin' with? You think I'm wet behind the ears?'

'What are you saying, mister?' The gambling man stayed his hands over the prize and rose to his feet as the room fell silent and the other players discreetly scraped their chairs back.

'I'm sayin' I won that pot fair and square. I'm sayin' you're a cheat and a liar. A stinkin', pimpin' . . . '

A silver-enscrolled, two-inch-barrelled derringer appeared in the gambler's hand from out of his sleeve and he held it unwaveringly on Crandal. 'Jest take them words back and get outa here — '

A shot barked out from the end of the bar spinning the gambling man in his tracks. He stood, poised, staring at the cloud of black powdersmoke from out of which the red-haired Finnegan appeared, his revolver raised, thumbed for a second shot.

Blam! The twelve-gauge roared as the gambler hit the deck. Crandal and Estevez hurled themselves to either side away from the scatter shot.

Ker-ash! Slim Soames, the owner, raised his revolver and his slug smashed the whiskey bottle out of Finnegan's grasp.

Pee-oww! A bullet whined from the balcony where Slippery Williams stood, his carbine smoking. It thudded into Soames' back and he slumped across his own bar.

Pa-dang! John Dog fired from where he had rolled on the floor and his lead sent Little Joe toppling from his high chair as simultaneously he released his second barrel.

Girls screamed as a big glass chandelier and pieces of plaster collapsed from the shot-peppered ceiling upon them. The barkeep came up with another shotgun but before he could fire El Cuchillo's knife sped through the air and cut a bloody groove through his bald head to send him crashing back on his bottles.

Slippery jerked his carbine lever and pumped lead into the dying men to finish them, as Seedy Smith came running out of a room on the landing in his filthy long johns and fired his revolver at all and sundry, sending a skinny prairie nymph, one Sally Simpson, to an early grave in the process.

In the sudden silence, after thirty seconds of slaughter, the five outlaws stood, their weapons at the ready, waiting for any others who cared to try them — but there were no offers. John Dog Crandal gave a wild grin, leaned over the table and scooped up the gold coin and dollars, thrusting them into his coat pockets. 'This here's rightly mine,' he said.

'What's going on?' a voice boomed out.

It was a big-bellied man, a badge of office pinned to his check shirt, sleeves rolled up over a red wool vest. He had braces and a thick belt holding up his baggy pants which were tucked into mud-grimed boots. Abe Ferguson was toting a carbine loosely in one hand. He looked around at the overturned chairs and smashed mirrors, the expensive chandelier on the floor, some of its candles still alight. 'Somebody better throw a bucket of water over that 'fore it sends the place up.'

He strode through the scene of carnage and studied each sprawled body, the bouquets of red beginning to flower through their clothes, the girl with a bullet through her throat, the 'keep with a knife in his head. With one hand he held Slim Soames up off the bar. His head lolled, his eyes were glazed. The sheriff let him slump back again. He turned the shotgun over with his boot. 'Li'l Joe,' he muttered. 'Looks like you got fired. You sure didn't do your job quick enough.' He looked down at the frozen features of the gambling man, even paler now as the blood seeped out of him. 'He's thrown his last ace. So' — he met Crandal's eyes — 'you been havin' some fun, have you?'

'That lousy skunk tried to cheat me. I called him. He drew that li'l popgun on me. Before we knew what was happenin' the damn shotgun was blasted at us. What you expect me an' my friends to do?'

The sheriff looked around and up at the balcony where Seedy and Slippery stood, their guns in their hands. 'So, they're friends of yourn, are they, mister? Seems to me like you know how to handle yourselves. You professional gunmen, by any chance?'

John Dog shrugged and grinned, as he thrust his revolver back in his belt. 'Not us. We're just hard-workin' cowboys. We were lookin' for a li'l quiet recreation in this town. We done anythang against the law?'

Abe Ferguson turned to the other men in the bar, who were finding their hats, stamping out the candles of the chandelier, and generally regaining their composure. 'Whoo!' one whistled. 'You ever see shootin' like that? Poor ole Slim bit off more than he could chew this time.'

'Is that the way it was? Are these gentlemen innocent victims of circumstance?'

'Yeah.' Men nodded and growled assent. 'The dealer drew first. It was a fair fight.'

'Right. I guess I ain't got nobody to arrest. That saves me some paperwork. Looks to me like this place will have to be put up for public auction. Might make a bid for it myself. Pity about young Sally. Anybody know if she got kin? No? Just a homeless whore, I guess. That's the way it goes. I'll git the undertaker to come measure up. Meantime, I guess I'll have to act as official receiver and see how much they got in the till and look in their safe. Sorry, folks, I'm gonna have to close this place down for tonight. Go find some other place to drink.'

As the people trooped out of the Ace-in-the-Hole, Ferguson looked over at the five outlaws. 'I'm warning you gents. Don't go getting in any more trouble in my town. I ain't gonna be so lenient next time.'

Crandal smiled and slapped his broad soft shoulder. 'Doncha worry, Sheriff. We ain't the troublesome type.'

9

Luke Hanlon's fur-chapped knees jutted out gawkily as he sat and leaned his leather-clad elbows on the back of a wooden chair. He gazed morosely at Matt Matthews who was propped up on his bearskin couch. 'Waal, I done all I can. Me and your boys been away eight days scouring the hills and on down to Troublesome. There ain't no sign of 'em.'

'No sign of the meat they stole? That was worth a coupla thousand dollars. It don't just disappear into thin air.'

'Murphy at the meat mart showed me receipts for everything. He said he's had no double dealings with nobody.'

'Well, he would, wouldn't he?'

'All I can do is take his word. Beef got no brand on it. Could be anybody's.'

'What about that lazy lummox, the

so-called Sheriff Ferguson? What did he have to say?'

'Nothing suspicious. No sign of rustling. The only trouble he'd had was a shoot-out at the Ace-in-the-Hole. He reckons Slim Soames brought it on himself. Him and three of his men got gunned down. They got caught at their cheating games.'

'Slim and three others? All dead? Whoever did it must have moved fast. Slim knew the score.'

'The sheriff reckoned it was a fair fight. Five *hombres* he had never seen before. Slim's boys started it so he let 'em go.'

'He would, wouldn't he?'

'Maybe he had no option. From all accounts they were real mean *hombres*. Sided each other, struck as fast as rattlers, killed with their first shot, mostly. One of the gals caught lead, too.'

'A gal? That would have been reason for holding them.'

'Accidental. She jest got in the way.

Unlucky, but that's the risk them sorta gals take. Jest a two-buck hoo-er. Nobody knew where she come from.'

'And nobody recognized those men?'

'Plenty of speculation. One fella reckons it was the Crandal gang. The leader was tall, bearded, shifty-looking. He had burn blotches on his face, so that ties in with Mary. It musta been him who was here.'

'So, where did they go to, these five mean *hombres*? Anybody any idea?'

'You know what Troublesome's like, Matt. Everybody clammed up soon as I started asking questions. They don't want to get involved when it comes to desperadoes like that. And Abe Ferguson ain't inclined to git off his butt to protect anyone. Like I say, we've raked through the hills but there's no sign. What more can I do?'

'No man could do more, Luke. I'm obliged to you.' Matt groaned as he tried to move his stiff leg and raise himself. Maybe, he thought, it was just as well Luke, Caleb and Elijah didn't have a run in with the Crandal gang. They would have been no match. These killers would have made mincemeat of them. So how was he to . . . ?

'Aw, Gawd!' he groaned. 'Why did I bump into that durn wolverine? When am I goin' to git outa this pit? Hand me that stick, will ya, Luke? You ready to see Mary into Oglala?'

'Where's she goin', Matt? All the way back East?'

'That's right. Stage leaves Oglala for Cheyenne in the mornin', don't it?'

'I mean, why's she goin'? It don't seem right, a time like this. A wife's place is behind her man. It seems like she's runnin' out on you, takin' the boy an' all.'

Matt winced, but whether it was with pain, or what, Luke wasn't sure. The rancher's steel-grey eyes met his as he beckoned him with outstretched fingers to tone his voice down.

'Sorry, I didn't think she could hear.'

Matt spoke in a lowered voice. 'She's gone into her shell since what happened. She didn't like the way the *Oglala Tribune* went on about how Jed ought to get a reward. Tryin' to make out the boy was some kinda hero.'

'Why in hell not? He was.'

'Mary don't want him growin' up like that. She thinks it best she should go away. She's got an idea she's gotta act in the interests of the boy's future. Once a woman's got an idea like that in her head there's no way of talkin' her outa it. Not that she's spoke much. Deep inside she's real upset.'

'Yeah, but what about her marriage vows?'

'I ain't gonna hold that over her. Anyway, I think it's for their own safety they go away. This Crandal, if it is Crandal, he ain't gonna forget that my boy killed one of his men, that Mary scarred him for life. He'll be back, mark my words.'

Luke stared at the rancher; his friend, a man who had been the most fair and fearless lawman he had known. 'You sound as if you're scared of him.'

'I am. Scared for my wife and son. I'll be OK on my own. Mary's nursed me back to strength. I'll be back in the saddle in a coupla days. Hell, it ain't as if she's taking the boy away for good.'

'Ain't she . . . are you so sure?'

Matt bit his teeth into his lip as he struggled to his feet, blinked his eyes, and looked away. 'Get outa here!'

When the sheriff had gone he braced himself, leaned on his stick and limped after him. Mary met him, wrapped against the cold in her travelling shawl. 'Luke says he's ready to go. Are you all right?'

'Sure I'm all right. Thanks to you.'

She had been a solicitous nurse, but, somehow, an invisible screen had dropped between them since the shooting. Her blue eyes had lost their warmth, her cheeks their colour. In place of her sparkle was a cold determination. She had packed a small trunk and outside they were loading it on to a mare. 'We should be in Chicago in four days. Then go on down to the coast.'

'Yeah,' he said, gruffly. 'Don't forget to write.'

'How could I forget you, Matt? I'm sorry, I feel like I'm deserting you, but I've just got to be alone. I've got to get away. I've got to think.'

The rancher nodded glumly, and tried to hug her in one arm to give a kiss. But she avoided his lips, turning her face away, offering only the coldness of her cheek. 'Don't, Matt,' she whispered.

Outside Elijah helped her up to sit side-saddle on a quiet gelding. Matt hugged Jed to him. 'Take care of your mother,' he said.

Mary glanced at him, and pulled her horse away, not looking back, following Luke out of the ranch gate. Jed cantered on his pony after them, turning to shout and wave.

Matt stood on the porch of the cabin

and watched them go, watched until they had rounded a wooded spur of the hills. Suddenly they were gone. He looked around at the gloomy evergreens, listened to the echoing klunk of the axe as Caleb and Elijah began cutting lodgepole pines to roof the new cellar. What in hell good was it now? He hobbled back into the cabin. It seemed strangely empty and forsaken without his wife and son.

'How dare they?' he said, taking his Winchester '73 from the rack and checking the mechanism. 'How dare those bastards come between me and my family? How dare they try to destroy my living, ruin my life? I'll catch up with you, Crandal, if it's the last thing I do.' At that moment he no longer cared whether he lived or died.

★ ★ ★

A rider came charging out of the woods, leaping a fallen log, and careering on towards Sundown Jack. At first he thought it was a young fellow and then saw it was a girl dressed as a man. Lou! She had a shooting iron in her hand and a shot rang out whistling past his ear as he whirled Smoke in his tracks and turned back to face her. 'Who the hell you shootin' at?'

'You. That's just a warning.' She rode up and covered him with her revolver. 'What you doin' on our land?'

'Your land?' Jack looked around him at the vast domain of snowy grass skirted by pine-covered mountains. 'This is my land. This land belong to the Oglala Sioux if anybody has a right to it.'

'It don't any more. It belongs to my daddy. And we don't want nobody trespassing. What you snooping around for?'

Jack gave her a crooked grin and steadied his restless pinto. 'Why, you got something to hide? Where is your daddy and his men? Where they all gotten to?'

Lou shrugged, trying to look tough

in her straight-brimmed, low-crowned hat, her buckskin jacket, jeans and boots. 'They gone catchin' wolves.'

'Yeah? Which way?'

'North. Up through Medicine Creek. I been told to keep all interlopers off our land.'

'Seems to me I ain't the first. I seen tracks back at your ranch house. Looks to me like they came from along the Snake River and was heading this way. You seen 'em?'

'None of your business. Just some of the boys, I guess. Well, are you leaving, or not? Or do I have to put air through your insides?'

Sundown grinned more broadly. 'You wouldn't dare.'

'No? Who's gonna miss some 'breed? Jest turn that pony round and head back the way you come. You wanna try me?'

Sundown's eyes flickered over her, and he kneed his pinto, turning him as if to obey but going, instead in a complete circle, pushing her horse aside and making a grab at her gun arm, fast and lithe, throwing himself from his saddle on to her. There was an explosion as her fingers squeezed. The next thing she knew she was lying on her back in the snow, the 'breed on top of her.

For moments she could not speak, winded by the thud of the fall. The revolver was twisted from her grasp and tossed away. And then she felt him pressing himself into her, a bony knee prising her thighs apart. She was breathing heavily as she looked into his dark eyes. 'This the way I wanna try you,' Sundown bared his white teeth, his black hair hanging down touching her smooth cheeks. 'How 'bout you?'

Lou did not speak for moments, her heart pounding frantically. Then she came to her senses. 'Get off me. My daddy'll kill you he finds out. He hates all Injins and 'breeds.'

'Yeah, how many Apache did he kill? How many southern Rebs, the big hero?'

Sundown Jack gave a mirthless laugh as he scowled down at her, then lay aside to let her rise. Lou retrieved her hat, brushing herself down, trying to salvage her dignity. She went to pick up her gun but Sundown rolled over and was there before her. He stood and emptied the cylinder, scattering the bullets away. 'I ain't sure I trust you.'

He handed the nickel-plated .38 back and she stuffed it into her belt. She stuck out her fleshy lower lip, belligerently, pulled her hat down over her fringe, grabbed hold of her horse and swung into the saddle. 'I'm telling you again to get off this land — for your own good. And don't come back.'

Sundown watched her as she rode away, and grinned, sardonically. 'A cute li'l filly, eh, Smoke? Pity about her pa. I wonder where she's off to? One way to find out.'

He cantered the pinto along at a discreet distance following her tracks in the snow and, after some while, was passing an outcrop of rocks. He was studying the ground instead of the trees when the shadow of a rope dropped over him, the rawhide tightening around his shoulders, and with an abrupt twang he was jerked back out of the saddle.

He looked up, the breath knocked out of him, and saw Lou, the rope tied tight to her saddle horn. He tried to wrest it from his shoulders, but she spurred her horse and pulled him to his knees. 'You don't take good advice, do you?' She kneed her horse into a run, dragging him bouncing along the ground. Sundown tried to grab the rope with his free hands but he was twisting and bouncing through the rough ground and considerably shaken up by the time she pulled in near a cabin.

Lou jumped down and her horse took the strain of the man as if he were some thrown steer. She jammed the nickel-plated barrel into Jack's neck and said, 'You think I'd go out without a few spare slugs in my pocket?'

'I guess,' he gasped, 'I underestimated you.'

'You sure did, cowboy.' Lou neatly wound the rope tight around his shoulders until his hands were pinned. She relieved him of his Colt and his hunting knife, cut the rope and knotted him tight, all the time keeping the cold barrel pressed to his neck in case he should kick out. 'Got you trussed like a turkey for the oven. Now git in there.'

The small cabin beneath the pines was used by her father's linesmen. She jabbed the gun into Sundown's back and pushed him inside. 'Get on the floor.'

'You gonna shoot me if I don't?'

'You can have it now or later, please yourself.'

Sundown gave her a lecherous grin and sank cross-legged to the plank floor. 'Depends what you're talkin' 'bout.'

Lou had another rope over her shoulder which she quickly looped about his ankles and pulled tight hoisting him to tie it to a solid six-inch nail in the wall. She slung one end as a noose around his throat and tied that to a post of the bunk. 'There,' she grunted, jerking the rope back and forth and tying numerous knots. 'Get outa that.'

'Hey,' Jack protested. 'Thass damn tight. I'm gonna lose the circulation in my hands, not to speak of my head.'

'That ain't all you'll lose.' Lou knelt down to him with an insidious smile on her lips, the razorsharp knife in her hand. She touched it to his lower parts. 'You're mighty proud of that thang of yours in your pants, aincha? You try pressing that into me again I'll be fryin' it for breakfast.'

'Whoo!' A mite uncomfortable, he tried to wriggle away but it was impossible. She had got him hog-tied. 'You're quite a gal. I shoulda thought twice 'fore tangling with you.'

'You surely should, darlin'.' She smiled at him, relishing her power, and put her soft-cheeked face close, sticking out her pink tongue, and giving a mocking lick an inch from his lips. 'What you Injins do, anyway? Rub noses or kiss lips?'

'Depends which side of me's operatin' — a French kiss or a Sioux rub.'

'For a 'breed you sure got a lot of lip.'

'You ain't gonna leave me here? I thought you was playin'.'

'If you don't freeze to death my daddy'll have a hanging party when he gets back. Nobody touches his baby gal.'

'Lou, you wouldn't want to get mixed up in that. It'd be mighty lonesome in a prison cell. And them uniform stripes wouldn't look well. I can think of mightier pleasanter things me and you could do.'

'Shut up. I gave you your chance to get out.' She checked the ropes were tight. 'Pleasant dreams, Sundown Jack.'

10

The days passed in a strange calm. There was never a night that there was not a fall of snow, but it left only a thin layer, nothing to worry about for the cattle could poke through it to the grass. There was hardly a breath of wind, as if the world had ceased turning. It increased Matt's sense of isolation, alone in the cabin, and his apprehension about his uncertain future. He had an awful sensation in the pit of his stomach that he would never see his wife and son again. He occupied himself trying to exercise his damaged leg, forcing himself to walk back and forth without the stick. The wound in his neck had healed, the stitches long since taken out. But sometimes he felt as if it had somehow affected his sight. It would hit him out of the blue, a dizziness, a blurred vision, as if he was going to fall, but he would force himself to control it. If he stood and got a grip on himself he could get over it. It happened as he tried to get back on a horse for the first time. It was bad enough getting his stiff leg over the saddle, and then it hit him. But he managed to stay in the saddle.

'Mister Matthews! Mister Matthews!' Caleb came racing into the ranch across the snowy pasture, the split tails of his duster coat flapping, quirting his bronc for all he was worth as if the Sioux were after him. He slithered to a halt and pointed a finger back. 'They've struck again. Along towards Snake Bend.'

Matt sat his horse and snapped, 'How many?'

'A good hundred head taken. There's tracks of horsemen. A tidy bunch of 'em.'

'Where's Elijah?'

'I left him there while I come to raise the alarm.'

'Where's Jack!'

'Huh, I dunno. One minute he's

here, the next he's gone. I never know where that fella is.'

Don't say he's run out on me, too, Matt thought, with a stab of self-pity. He jutted his square jaw, grey as granite, and called, 'You got plenty ammo? Catch a fresh hoss. Let's grab some vittles and blankets and git after 'em.'

'You fit enough, Mister Matthews?'

'How many times I tell you to call me Matt? 'Course I'm fit. Don't hang about, man.'

'You ain't been out before. It'll be a long ride. You sure you — '

'I tell you — less git.'

★ ★ ★

They rode at a steady lope along the banks of the Snake until they came to a pasture close to the big bend of the river. They found Elijah sitting on a rock. He had made a small fire and had coffee boiling. He handed up his boss a mug of the steaming tarry liquid.

'Seen anything?' Matt asked, grasping the mug, grateful for the warmth. The long ride had taken a lot out of him.

'Not a soul.'

'We took a tally of the cows in this valley two days ago. All prime stock. The best we got. All gone. I'll show you the tracks,' Caleb said. 'It looks like they forded 'em over the river and headed across the captain's land.'

'Captain Herb Newton,' Matt muttered, staring across the wide placid river. He tossed the coffee dregs away and passed the mug to Caleb. 'Git some heat inside you, an' we'll go see what he's got to say.'

They doused the fire, climbed back on their horses and gritted their teeth as they plunged through the icy water It was a shallow enough crossing but they could not avoid getting their legs and thighs wet. It was dusk by now, but they could see that the trail of the beeves and horsemen went at an angle

144

by-passing by a mile or so the captain's ranch house.

As they followed it Captain Newton hove into sight, a familiar figure in his faded cavalry outfit and white moustache. He had two outriders, shabby men, with the look of down-at-heel punchers. 'What do you want?' he shouted. 'What are you doing on my land? Where are you going?'

'Where do you think we're going? We're following this trail of cattle.'

'Oh, it's you, Matthews.' Herb drew up and squinted at him through the dusk. 'Trail of cattle? Oh, I see. That's strange. Where have they come from?'

'They've come from my side of the river. They're my best stock. They been rustled. It's where they're going to I'm interested in. Didn't you see or hear nuthin'?'

'No, me and the boys have been up towards Medicine Creek hunting wolves. We jest got back. These varmints musta somehow heard we were away.'

'You sayin' you ain't seen nuthin'? And you ain't had none of your own stole?'

'No, we haven't I'm glad to say. We lost too many last winter to be able to afford any more losses. None of ours are gone. This gang seems to have a grudge against you, Matthews.'

'Yeah, they do. Like they're tryin' to wipe me out. Well, they ain't going to.'

One of the captain's men looked up from under his hat, sullenly. 'Lou said she saw that 'breed hangin' about.'

'Sundown Jack?'

'Yeah. She told him to clear off.'

'Maybe,' Caleb hooted, 'he's still in with this gang. He's allus disappearin'. Maybe he tips 'em off when the coast's clear. I never trusted him.'

'Yuh,' Elijah agreed. 'We shoulda let the posse string him up.'

Matt shook his head. 'I don't know. I don't think so.'

'Once an outlaw always an outlaw,' Newton grunted. 'You can tell him from me if I ever see him on my land again I'll shoot on sight.'

Caleb spat into the snow. 'You cain't trust 'em — 'breeds.'

'Come on,' Matt said. 'We'll follow this trail until it gets too dark to see. An' tomorrow we'll follow it some more. If you've no objection, Captain.'

'No,' he blustered. 'Go ahead. I'm just sorry I can't spare anyone to help you.'

'We'll fight our own battles,' Matt gritted out. 'There'll be a reckoning one day.'

★ ★ ★

Matt Matthews gasped at the pain in his leg as he cast aside his snow-crusted blanket in the dim light of dawn and tried to poke life into the fire, to get some life into his frozen mitts. Elijah went looking for kindling as Caleb got the coffee pot and frying pan on. Matt went to give his horse some split-corn and to sling on his saddle. When he

147

bent to tighten the double-cinch his head whirled so he nearly fell. He hung on to the beast to keep himself steady.

'What's wrong, Matt?' Caleb called.

'Nuthin'.' Matt shook his head, trying to focus.

'It ain't nuthin'.'

'I tol' you you weren't up to this.'

'Mebbe you were right,' Matt whispered. 'Come on, let's git some grub inside us and follow that trail 'fore it's all covered up. Ain't that coffee boiled yet?'

They moved off in the early dawn, although there was no sign of the sun, the sky a grey mist above them. There had been another thin fall of snow, making it difficult to see the tracks of the herded cattle, especially when they climbed over rocky ground where the cloven hooves made few indentations.

'Where'n hell they got to now?' Caleb shouted, searching the ground.

They had reached a maze of coulées and steepsided ravines and had to make a guess at which one the rustlers had entered. By noon, when the sun had become a faint glimmering lemon in the mist, they had explored three of them without success. All they saw were bighorn sheep high on the slopes, an eagle soaring with a lamb in its talons, and once a yellow mountain lion that leapt from a rock and dashed away.

'They could have 'em hidden in any of these damn box canyons. Which one shall we try next? Is there any way through to the other side of these mountains?'

'I dunno. It ain't much explored,' Caleb said. 'And it certainly ain't mapped.'

'It's like a damn maze,' Matt said. 'Come on, we'll try up this aways. Blaze a trail with your axe, Elijah. We don't want to git ourselves lost.'

★ ★ ★

Sundown Jack's body shuddered with cold. He had lain on the plank floor all night, his limbs constricted, stiffly. He had tried getting out of the ropes, twisting his head, trying to bite at them, but she had got him tied tight. She knew her knots, that girl. Finally, he had given up the struggle, resigned himself, tried to put his mind on a higher level, to ignore the pain and discomfort. But that was hard. He wondered about her, her soft brown eyes, her slim neck, the pursing of her lips when she tried to act tough, the warm swell of her body those few moments when he was pressed to her. A get-away-a-little-closer kind of feel. She was a wild one. But she couldn't be all bad. Could she? 'Hell take her,' he growled, trying to keep some movement in his hands. 'Mebbe she wants to see me dead. White folks sure is funny.'

It must have been mid-morning when he heard hoof-beats and the jingle of harness and Lou pushed through the door. 'Waal,' she grinned, 'if it ain't the 'breed. Have a good night?'

'Where's the necktie party?' he snarled. 'Or you jest come to torture me with the sight of that beautiful body?'

'Still got your lip?' She kicked at him with her pointed boot. 'You want me to leave you another night here? So, you just forget them kinda words. I ain't beautiful. And I certainly ain't gonna be no man's hoo-er. Not nobody's. An' certainly not yours. So you can get that idea outa your head.'

'Sure, boss. I'se already forgot. You jest a reg'lar guy.'

She used his knife to cut him free, and he pulled himself up, painfully, stomping his moccasined feet and soothing his wrists. His eyes met hers and he gave a mocking smile. 'What about your daddy?'

'He's gawn. The coast's clear. Get out.'

'And what about the other boys?'

'What other boys?'

'The ones whose tracks I saw.'

'I don't know what you're talking

about. Think yourself lucky I'm settin'
you free.'

He sat on the bunk and gave a low
whistle through his teeth as he looked
at her. 'Sweet as a prairie rose!'

'Cut the crap. Here!' She tossed him
his knife and his revolver. 'That ugly
li'l pony of yours is outside. You'll
probably find that stoopid tall hat you
wear back where I lassooed you.'

'Wouldn't want to lose a good hat.'

'Go on. Clear out.'

She was in the saddle of her fine
chestnut by the time he followed her
out, stomping the ground, ready to go.

'Lou!' he called.

'What?'

'Thanks.' He watched her tighten her
lips, give a blink of her eyes, rake her
spurs, and go shooting away towards
her father's ranch. 'Thassall.'

★ ★ ★

'It's Sundown Jack,' Caleb hollered,
pulling his carbine from the saddle boot.

'That lowdown 'breed. I'd recognize that ragtail pony of his anywhere.'

'Hold your fire,' Matt shouted, as he saw the half-Indian coming towards them across a snow-flat on a crag-side. 'Just keep him covered, Caleb.'

'Howdy,' Jack called as he approached.

'Howdy to you, you belly-slidin' rat,' Caleb said.

'Where's the rest of 'em?'

'The rest of who?'

'Them lousy rustlers you in with, who else?'

Sundown Jack shrugged his broad shoulders and a grin split his dark face. 'Ain' you found 'em? Thought you was on their tail. Thass why I'se followin' you.'

'Where you bin, Jack?' Matt asked.

'I bin tied up, boss. Miss Lou extended her hospitality, you might say. Couldn't git away. Weren't perlite.'

'What's he talkin' about?' Caleb retorted, cocking his carbine, aiming at Jack's chest.

'He's lyin',' Eijah said.

'I ain't lyin', boss. I bin indisposed for twenty-four hours.' He showed his reddened wrists. 'Forcefully, you might say. She's a bit of a disciplinarian is Miss Lou.'

'You know anything about my rustled cows?'

'No more than you. Jest them hoof-tracks. Take it you ain't found 'em.'

'They've disappeared into thin air again.' The rancher studied Jack and decided he was talking some kind of truth. 'Stop pointin' that gun at him, Caleb.'

'What? You lettin' him go?'

'Mebbe I can find 'em, boss. I know some of their hidey-holes.'

Caleb spat with disgust. 'He'll jine 'em, thass what he'll do.'

'We're going back,' Matt said. 'Before they git their hands on the rest of my stock. To tell the truth I ain't feelin' so hot. Ain't up to long-ridin' jest yet.'

'Take it easy, boss. I'll go take a look-see on my own. Thet OK with you?'

Matt nodded and pulled his bear coat close against the cold that shivered his body. 'Take care. Don't do anything foolish. You locate their hideout you come straight back. I'll git Luke Hanlon to raise a posse.'

'Sure, boss.' Sundown touched a finger to his black hat, and nudged his pony on past them. 'So long.'

11

'No wonder your poor hands are so red and roughened, my dear,' Agatha Feavoir exclaimed, placing her manicured ones over Mary's knuckles. 'Do you mean to say you did your own washing and sewing. Didn't you have any maidservants?'

'And my own cooking, weaving, milking and butter-making, too,' Mary said, drawing her hands away, somewhat guiltily. 'The wilds of Wyoming are a long way from civilization's niceties.'

'This cabin you lived in?' Alfred Quain said. 'I presume you just took it for the summer?'

'No, all weathers. It was all we had. My husband, Matt, built it with his own hands. Of course, we had a couple of barns and a bunkhouse.'

'A bunkhouse!' Kitty Carty gave

a shrill giggle. 'It sounds positively antediluvian.'

Mary looked around her at the social gathering, ladies in their coiffed hair, jewels and satin dresses, the gentlemen in formal evening wear, and wondered why she was being made to feel ashamed of her life in the West, why she was speaking about it as if it were past and over.

'Your father's works are in constant demand.' Gordon Freak saw her embarrassment and changed the subject. 'We are bringing out a new edition.'

'A pity his ideas weren't recognized for their worth when he was alive,' Mary told the publisher — he had thrown this dinner party for her at his town house in Boston.

'Alas, it is often the case. A writer suddenly finds fame, even immortality, after his demise. His, I understand, was a long hard struggle.'

'It was. Very long and very hard. And mostly unrewarded.'

'Well, you, my dear, may now reap

the benefit,' Freak said. 'Who better to edit a life of the great humanitarian than his daughter? And we're hoping you may find some unfinished opus among his papers. Or even early unpublished works. We want to see it all.'

'Is that Granpa?' Jed asked. 'Is he going to be famous?'

Mary smiled at him and stroked his blond fringe out of his eyes. 'I think he well may be.'

'I knew it,' Jed told them. 'My ma knows lots of stuff an' she learnt it all from Gramps. Nobody knows as much as my ma.'

There was a titter of amusement among the women, who began chattering among themselves. Freak took the opportunity to approach closer. He was not an unhandsome man, with an unruly head of greying curls, given a certain haughtiness by his monocle. He had to constrict his facial muscles to keep it in place. 'Do I take it you are separated from your husband?' he asked, squinting down at Mary's ample bosom in her low-cut gown.

'No!' she exclaimed. 'Not exactly. No, of course not. I just had to get away, that's all.'

'Madam, I am not surprised you departed. A lady of breeding and intelligence living like some emigrant. You're not thinking of going back to live in your shack in the wilds?'

'I — ' Mary was at a loss for words, looking down at her hands in her lap — workwoman's hands. 'I really don't know what I'm going to do.'

'But, Mary — may I call you that?' Freak said. 'There's so much here in Boston for you to do. So many people who want to meet you. So much work for us both to do.'

'Why should people want to meet me? It was my father who wrote those books.'

'And you were his mainstay. Perhaps there is more of you in his work than you are given credit for.'

Alfred Quain, also adjusted his

spectacles to get a better view of Mary, while Major McQuorkindale questioned the boy in an avuncular way. 'So what made you up-sticks and leave the prairies, young man?'

'I had to. I shot and killed a man.'

His words rang out in a sudden lull in conversation and the room fell silent.

McQuorkindale snorted over his sherry. 'Killed a man?'

'Yes, he was hurting my ma. I had to.'

'You mean, you allowed this child to carry a gun out there?' Daisy Oliphant asked Mary.

'The gun was for rabbits.' Mary was flustered. 'It was an accident. He didn't mean to.'

'I did,' Jed shouted. 'I'd do it again. And my dad's gonna catch up with them other badmen and gun them down, too.'

'Jed!' Mary shouted, but fortunately at that point a flunkey entered to announce the serving of dinner.

'I am not surprised you had to leave,' Mr Freak murmured as he escorted Mary in on his arm.

★ ★ ★

'OK, ladies and gents, going, going, gone for two hundred and fifty dollars to Mr John Crandal.' Sheriff Ferguson stood on the stage of the Ace-in-the-Hole and banged the butt of his revolver like a hammer. 'This fine saloon, liquor, glasses, gaming tables and girls all included. Oh, yeah, an' the piano player.'

The handful of citizens who had made bids muttered, glumly, and turned aside. They had been dissuaded from bidding against Crandal by the meaningful scowls of his villainous crew, who leaned or sat on the stage and watched them. The Mex was slapping a knife against his palm; Slippery Williams spinning his revolver back and forth on one finger.

'If you come backstage you can sign

the deeds,' Ferguson said, and, when they were out of earshot, told John Dog, 'That was a piece of cake. Here, sign here. We're partners, only I don't want nobody to know I'm involved.'

Crandal grinned and scrawled his sign. 'Me, the boss of a saloon. Who woulda thought it? My old mother would turn in her grave.'

'I cain't imagine you ever had one.' The sheriff offered his hand to shake. 'Here's my paw on it. The four of us are partners now. Between us we'll take over this town, buy up all the best land in the district once your boys have forced the ranchers to their knees. Stick with me, John Dog, and you'll start to make real money. Nobody will be able to prove it ain't legal.'

'The four of us?'

'Yeah, I run the town, you the Ace, your mugs do the dirty work, rustle the steak, Murphy processes the beef, gets a good price for it, and our other friend gives what assistance is necessary. We split the dividends four ways after paying the boys their peanuts.'

'I got a free hand how I run this joint?'

'Sure, as long as you don't go gittin' trigger-happy. We don't want any of them US deputy marshals to come pokin' their noses in. Jest keep a happy house with a crooked table and make sure there ain't too much trouble.'

John Dog smiled and patted the .45 in his belt. 'Don't worry about that, Ferguson. Nobody ain't gonna make trouble with me and my bunch about.'

'That's what I'm relyin' on. Remember, you gotta make receipts of everything you buy and sell. You're in business now, Crandal. Us partners will want to take a look at your books.'

'Don't you worry none about that. We'll make a profit.' Crandal gave a wild whoop and tucked the deeds in his pocket. 'And we're gonna start right now.'

He strode back into the saloon and looked across at the new 'shotgun', the barman he had already hired, at the cluster of girls sitting about painting their fingernails, kind of bored.

'Right, you li'l angels of delight,' John Dog shouted. 'I'm your new boss and here's the set-up. You charge the clients four dollars a throw from now on, three dollars to me and a dollar for yourselves.'

'No, that ain't right!' The leading chorette, Hetty L'Amour, pouted her cupid-bow lips, and stroked out the ringlets of her blonde wig. 'We're artistes, singers, dancers, not just common hookers. We were gettin' half of what we made afore. That's the way it should be.'

'You git one dollar now on. You'll have to work overtime to make up any shortfall. Understood?' John Dog hooked his thumbs in his belt and glowered at Hetty. 'And me and my boys git serviced for free any so time we feel like it.'

'Hell, no.' Hetty faced him, arms akimbo, her breasts jutted out in two aggressive points by her tight corset beneath the skimpy gown. 'Sally Simpson was a friend of mine. I ain't havin' nuthin' to do with that swine' — she pointed at Seedy Smith. 'He murdered her with his wild shooting.'

'No, nor me,' another girl chimed in, scratching at the crotch of her red flannel drawers. 'Sally was a nice kid.'

'If you other four wan' us you gotta pay the same as any other punter,' Hetty said. 'That's the deal.'

'I see we got a troublemaker. Right, you come with me, darlin'.' He grabbed hold of her, slung her like a bag of potatoes over his shoulder and, with her screaming, kicking, and banging her little fists, carried her unceremoniously up the stairs. On the landing he turned, keeping a tight hold, and shouted, 'I'm taking my first free feel as owner. Git them roulette wheels turning, the whiskey flowing, the piano playing and you gals git on stage and start dancin' to earn your supper. Bring the customers in and begin enjoyin' yourselves. We

165

got money to make.'

John Dog strode into a bedroom, threw Hetty bouncing on to a mattress. As she sat up, he backhanded her across the jaw, snapping her head back. He laid aside his revolver, unbuckled his heavy leather belt and slapped it cracking across a chair. 'Looks like I gotta teach you to behave.' Hetty's eyes opened wide with fear and she cringed, trying to back away, but he had her by one arm, twisting her over as the belt whistled through the air. 'Take that, you bitch,' he grinned. 'By the time I'm finished with you you ain't gonna be able to sit down for days.'

★ ★ ★

Even though there was a new fall of snow on the ground Sundown Jack did not have great difficulty following the trail of the rustled cattle for he knew the way the gang operated, splitting the herd into small bunches, going north, then south, crossing and recrossing until anybody who did manage to follow one spoor was almost put into a paroxysm of rage by encountering others going in the opposite direction. Sundown knew how to cross that maze of mountains and had a rough idea where they were going. He was so intent on seeking his way through he did not notice he was being followed.

His hunch paid off for towards late afternoon of the third day, the winter dusk quickly closing in, he reached the rim of a south-facing canyon and heard the soft bellowing of cattle. There they were, a good hundred longhorns, most plainly marked with the big double M brand. And there were a couple of his former *compadres*, Estevez and Slippery Williams, standing at the camp-fire, while three nondescript 'punchers he didn't recognize — or did he? — rode bounds, guarding the exit of the box canyon and keeping a lookout.

Sundown Jack left his pinto on the far side of the ridge and wriggled forward on his belly through the prickly scrub keeping an eye cocked for any other invigilators. He had his carbine in his hand and he peered along the sights estimating whether he could take the two ringleaders out before the others took cover. Hadn't he warned them, let them go with that stolen meat, warned them not to come back and prey on Matthews again? One warning ought to be enough for any man. An anger in him urged him to take out those two round the fire immediately, but he held back. It was almost darkness. They would be tricky shots. And, again, he had little stomach for back-shooting, however necessary.

He watched them for a good while until all he could see was the flickering fire and the silhouettes of men as they passed back and forth. He could smell the hot soup they were supping and his belly rumbled. He chewed on some dried jerky and took a mouthful of ice-cold water from his wooden canteen. He tried to think of a plan to retrieve the stolen cattle, but it looked like all he could do come daylight was ride in guns blazing. 'There's gonna be lead for breakfast one way or t'other,' he muttered, as he dodged back down the ridge to his pinto. He stumbled around in the dark and found a little walled-in, brush-covered chasm, got a grip on Smoke's neck and forced him to lie down. Jack wrapped his Indian saddle blanket around himself and lay down beside his pony for warmth. Soon he fell into an exhausted sleep.

When he woke it was the darkest hour before dawn. He felt under his saddle for his revolver where he had tucked it to keep it dry. Funny! He struck a match and looked everywhere, but it had gone. He spun around searching for his carbine. That, too, was missing. 'Things gittin' mighty peculiar around here.' He scratched at his thick black hair, at a loss. 'I sure weren't drunk. An' I ain't a believer in ghosts, waal, not the sort that takes your guns.'

Suddenly, he spotted prints of riding boots in the snow. 'I bin robbed! An' whoever done it sure got a dainty foot.'

He chuckled as he stamped some circulation into his feet, and fed his pony a handful of corn. There was no way he could take on the five rustlers without his guns. and maybe impossible to outgun them if he still had them. 'Waal, ain't this topsy-turvy? Seems like somebody don't want me to go git myself kilt. You don't reckon it could be thet li'l filly, do yuh, Smoke? But why for?'

It was still not yet light, only a glimmer of dawn in the eastern sky. Sundown climbed back to the rim to take another look. Four of the *hombres* were down there rolled up in their blankets about their fire looking mighty cosy. He spotted the sudden red pinprick of a cigarette and saw the shadowy shape of a fifth one on a horse. He was taking his turn guarding the cattle and keeping look-out. He had a poncho around his shoulders and his *sombrero* was silhouetted against the skyline.

'Estevez!' Well, if she thought she could stop him making his play she was wrong. There were other ways without guns. Sundown still had his knife. He had never liked El Cuchillo epecially since seeing him slit the throat of that ferryman's wife. The 'breed rolled over the rim and slid silently through the rocks and undergrowth towards the horseman. He hardly dared breathe for fear of startling the cattle. He eased his way around them, gradually getting nearer to the Mexican.

'Haiee! El Cuchillo!' he hissed out.

Estevez spun his horse to face him, his hand going instinctively to the knife under his armpit. Sundown Jack grinned at him. The knife was in the Mexican's hand, poised to throw. Too late. 'Ugh!' Estevez grunted with dismay as Sundown's big Bowie spun towards him, a flash in the night, and embedded in his chest.

Sundown Jack dodged forward and caught his horse as Estevez slumped from the saddle. With his other hand the 'breed caught him and eased him to the ground. The Mexican's cruel-cut features were already fixed in the rictus of death as Sundown took his double belt of ammunition, and his long-barrelled Hopkins and Allen XL army revolver, .44 calibre. 'Whew!' Jack gave a low whistle of admiration as he tried the mother-of-pearl birdclaw butt for size. 'Ain' never seen one like this afore.' He eased the rifle from the boot beneath the stirrup leather of the silver-studded saddle, and thrust it home again. He dropped the heavy ammunition belt to one side and hitched the horse to a rock. He jerked his knife from the Mexican's chest, wiped it in the snow clean of blood and slid it back into the sheath on his belt then went forward on foot towards the fire.

His moccasins made no sound as he crept towards Slippery, one of the wiliest badmen on the northern range. He was wrapped up in his greatcoat, his hat over his nose, under his blanket, his carbine held loosely in one hand. Sundown carefully eased it from him and pushed it behind a rock. He knew where Slippery kept his Colt six-shooter, in the capacious pocket of his greatcoat. He picked the blanket back and the gun from his pocket. He hid that, too.

There! He breathed more easily. That was the two most dangerous varmints with their teeth pulled. Sundown stepped over to the three other sleeping men. The sky had lightened with the upsurge of the sun's rays flickering across the horizon and he could see them clearly. The trouble was they could see him if they woke. One of them, his head slumped against his saddle, was wearing his revolver in its studded holster on his hip. As Sundown reached for the walnut butt the man groaned and opened his eyes. 'What in hell's goin' on?' Sundown had it out and thudded him across the jaw with it.

He turned to the other two men. One of them had sat up, a carbine in his hands and Sundown saw the flash of fire as the slug whistled out. In the same split second he rolled aside and tried to fire the Hopkins from lying on the ground — but it jammed. Somehow he hadn't got the hang of the safety catch. Jeezis! he thought. The cowboy was levering his carbine for a second shot and it looked to Sundown that his time had come.

'Kill him!' Slippery Williams shouted, as he felt around in panic for his own missing guns.

The cowboy gritted his teeth and aimed at the 'breed who tried to roll away. As he did so a shot cracked out from the hillside. The cowboy cried out in pain and crumpled. He fell over the carbine which exploded ear-shatteringly.

The third stranger, a surly-looking jackanapes, had his .45 out ready to put a slug in the 'breed. But he looked around anxiously when he heard the shot from the hillside and another slug spat past his head.

Sundown sprang to his feet covering him with the Hopkins, which was still jammed. 'Drop that, mister. Or you'll be dead meat like your buddy.'

Reluctantly, the man did as he was bid, tossing the revolver towards the fire. Sundown spun slowly round, watching the three of them. They didn't know he couldn't get the durn thing to fire. So they spread their hands.

'Thass better.' Sundown crouched down and looked up at the hillside. 'Who the hell's up there?'

A fringed buckskin coat, a purple bandanna, a flat-crowned hat, and tight pants clothing a slim, shapely figure showed itself, a rifle in one hand. She began to climb down the hillside through the snow-covered sage.

'Hi!' she called, cheerily. 'You got things under control?'

'My guardian angel.' Jack grinned at

Slippery. 'Whaddaya know!'

'What you done with my guns?' Slippery complained.

'A li'l trick she taught me. More to the point, what you doing with these cows?'

Lou reached the fire and swung her rifle at them, threateningly. 'You damn fool,' she said to Sundown. 'I thought I told you to clear out and go home.'

'What you doin' here?' Slippery demanded. 'What you do that to him for? He's one of your — '

'Shut up,' Lou snapped out at him. 'Unless you want a slug in you same as him.'

She rolled the cowboy over with her boot. 'Eugh! What a mess. I didn't really mean to kill him.'

'You didn't,' Sundown said. 'He fell on his own carbine. Blown half his face away.'

'What we gonna do with these three?' the girl asked. 'I guess I'm on your side now.'

'Waal, we could string 'em up, let

their boots kick air. It's what the polecats deserve. But two dead this time of the mornin's enough for my stomach. I figure we should send 'em on their way.'

'Two dead? You mean the Mex?' Slippery said.

'Yep. He got a taste of his own treatment — cold steel.'

The cattle were milling about, bellowing and fighting, frightened by the gunfire, but the outlaws had felled lodgepole pines across the entry to the canyon so they couldn't escape. The steers looked pretty mean and restless and Jack was worried they might make a rush for it. 'We got to settle these dogies down and head 'em back to the Matthews' range,' he said, glancing at the girl. 'Are you gonna help me do that?'

Lou shrugged. 'I guess so. Don't know what's gotten into me.'

The 'breed flashed a grin at her. 'How about you two?' he asked the cowpokes. 'You gonna give us a hand?'

'Why should we do that?' the one who had tossed his Colt away, asked truculently.

Sundown picked it up and stuck it in his belt. ' 'Cos it's mighty hard herdin' 'em on our own. An' cos iffen you do we gonna let you go scotfree. But, if you don't — '

The other one was ruefully rubbing his jaw where Jack had slugged him. 'Sounds fair enough.'

'Right, so first we'll bile up some coffee and have a bite of bacon. One of you stir some life into that fire.'

As they did so and prepared breakfast Sundown went and retrieved the Mexican's grey. 'Mighty fine bronc and Spanish rig,' he said. 'An' a real swell six-shooter. If only I knew how the durn thang worked.'

'You mean to say you couldn't fire that?' Lou laughed at the expression on his face as he puzzled over the Hopkins. 'You sure fooled these three. Look.' She took the weapon from him. 'See that? That's the safety catch.

Another notch forward operates the swing-out cylinder.' She deftly clicked it out, gave it a spin. 'Makes it easier for loading.'

'Jeez. Thet's the first one I see'd. What'll they think of next?'

'Try it.' She handed it back. 'State of the art.'

'What you done with my ole Frontier?'

'It's behind a rock. Howja know it was me?'

'Who else?'

'Don't flatter yourself. I jest didn' want to see you killed, thassall. If I hadn't been here you woulda been.'

They sat around munching on bacon and beans, swilling it down with coffee, keeping a wary eye on the unarmed men. Still chewing, Sundown climbed on the dead Mexican's horse. 'I'll go pick up my pinto.'

'What about me?' Slippery said.

'You? You got a long walk ahead of you. Back to Troublesome. You can tell them other coyotes to keep their hands off Mistuh Matthews' cattle.

Or else there really will be trouble. Come on, boys, let's git these dogies movin'.'

'Aincha gonna give me a hoss?' Slippery pleaded. 'Or a gun?'

'I sure ain't.' Sundown pointed his new Hopkins and Allen at him. 'Git movin'. Pronto! I don' wanna see your ugly mug agin.'

12

For days in late December came a succession of blizzards. None was as severe as the great blizzard of the previous January, but in aggregate they began to prove almost as deadly. They wore down the bodies and spirits of men, horses and stock. The blizzards were hitting the country further west that had escaped the storm of the winter before, and Wyoming was right in the midst of it. Matt and his men hacked their horses along through the hills and river valley trying to keep a watch on the stock. But it was obvious that more had disappeared. And there was only one way they could have been taken, across the flat prairie grass of Captain Herb Newton's land.

'You wan' me to go across keep a watch-out?' Sundown Jack's face was like a dark wooden mask. He narrowed his eyes against the falling snowflakes and hunched his shoulders as he sat his sturdy pinto. 'I ain't got nuthin' else to do.'

Matt gave an amused snort at the 'breed's drawled dismissal of danger, for dangerous it could be riding out there on his own. 'It wouldn't be the gal you're more interested in keeping an eye on, would it? Ain't Cap'n Herb threatened to kill you if you go sniffin' after her?'

'I'll take my chances,' Sundown grinned and twisted his pony away.

Matt watched him go riding off, he and his pinto one. He was a natural horseman, the best he had ever known, with an Indian's easy knack of staying in the saddle, as if glued there, whether the bronc shied or was spooked by some darting bobtail. The brittle cold did not bother him. He could read the signs, knew what the weather would do, stay alive in the wilds. Behind his strange way of speaking, his dry humour, was a man who was strong and resolute and always ready to take a chance.

'I don't know what we'd do without him,' he muttered, more to himself. 'I still cain't figure how he managed to bring them hundred head back all by hisself.'

'There was somethang fishy 'bout that,' Caleb said. 'He ain't tellin' all he knows.'

'Come on, Caleb, jest 'cause he admits to doin' a spot of rustling . . . if he ever figured to settle down to hard work in one place he'd be one of the best.'

'But he won't. He ain't a white man. He ain't like you an' me. You cain't trust 'breeds.'

'C'mon. Less git back to the ranch.

* * *

It surprised him how much work there was to do around the cabin now Mary had gone, the cows to milk and muck out, the ice to break for water, the wood to be brought in, the cooking and washing and tidying up — what tidying got done. And he had forgotten how lonesome it could be on his own as he sat in the creaking armchair by the stove, looked up and saw small things that reminded him of them, a cushion cover she had embroidered, the boy's toy bow and arrows. Through the long nights he sat and listened to a loose shutter banging mournfully, like the tolling of a bell, the distant howl of wolves, or the river ice creaking as it froze.

When he rode out along the river he kept a wary eye cocked for his enemy the wolverine, the Evil One, but saw no sign. He and the boys did what they could to rescue stock, riding out into the deep snows between the great frosted crags as windblown, stinging, granulated ice cut into their faces, turning Caleb's beard to icicles. When he got back to the cold cabin in the dusk Matt could not help succumbing to more moments of self-pity when he remembered its former warmth, the welcoming faces, the steaming meals and hot apple pies waiting for him. He thought, too, of Mary's body, her sensuous embrace, not this cold unmade bed that awaited him now.

Luke Hanlon rode over one day with a letter. He sat by the stove warming his hands and sipping from a mug of coffee as he watched Matt read. The rancher's square-jawed face had taken on a grim look. 'When's she coming home?' Luke asked.

In her neat script Mary rambled on about her father's neglected house, his books and papers she was involved in putting into order, some publisher, Gordon Freak, who had invited her to dinner parties and meetings.

Gordon has been very kind and enthusiastic, and old friends, Agatha Feavoir and Alfred Quain are regular visitors. They all ask about you . . . '

'I bet they do,' he muttered. He wasn't sure he liked the first-name term, Gordon, nor all the talk about social gatherings, nor the fact that Jed had been enrolled at school. It did not augur well to his ears. Indeed, it seemed more like a letter from some kind, but distant, relative, as if they had returned to a world far beyond him. She closed with an odd phrase, *'your devoted friend and wife'*, but there was no spontaneous expression of love or kisses.

He folded the letter and tucked it in his shirt pocket. 'What was that, Luke?'

'When's she coming back?'

'She don't exactly say.' Matt turned his chair away and lapsed into silence.

And Luke cleared his throat after a while and said, 'I guess I'd better be gittin' back.'

★ ★ ★

Sundown Jack spent days watching Captain Newton's range. At nights he returned to the little cabin in the woods where she had kept him prisoner. One day his watching bore fruit for he saw several riders approach the Newton's ranch. He threw himself from the saddle, dragging the pinto down with him. He crawled forward through a deep snowdrift and was relieved to see that he hadn't been spotted.

'John Dog Crandal,' he hissed through his teeth. 'What's he doin' here?'

And he recognized the burly shape of Slippery Williams in his long duster coat, the tatterdemalion Seedy Smith, and among their six companions were men he knew as lowdowns who hung around the frontier settlements, white trash who would back-shoot any man for the right price.

'Looks like he's got hisself a new gang together.'

It was getting near dark and another snowstorm had begun so, taking advantage of the terrain, rock outcrops and an overhang of pines, Sundown made his way towards the ranch. He hitched the pinto to a branch and scrambled down, making a crouching run towards the back of the outbuildings. He wriggled through a hole in a barn wall and the hooves of stabled horses, whispering to them to stay quiet. He peered out and across to the lit windows of Newton's cabin. There was a guard outside, holding a rifle, stamping his feet and blowing on his knuckles. When his back was turned Sundown slipped across and down the shadowed side of the cabin. He put his eye to an unchinked hole in the wall but could see only men's backs. He could hear the high-pitched aggressive whine of Crandal.

'It ain't jest his cows I want. I want to see him and that bitch of his dead. You see my face? Every time I see this in a mirror I think of what I'm goin' to do to her and that brat of her'n.'

'You're too late.' It was the deep drawl of Captain Newton. 'She's gawn. She's miles away back East. And I don't figure she's coming back.'

'Well, maybe if she hears that something real bad has happened to him, an' to her home, that'll bring her back?'

'Talk sense, man. So, she ruined your good looks? So what!' There was an outburst of laughter at that. 'I made it quite clear when I agreed to come in with you that I didn't want any unnecessary killing. All I want is Matthews' stock. I want to put him out of business. And I want his land. He had no right homesteading that land behind my back.'

'An' I tell you I need to be even with the Matthews' clan. What's it to you? You a frien' of ther'n?'

'No, I'm not. But they're decent folk and there ain't no need for killin'. You got what you asked for for tangling with that woman in the first place.'

'Tanglin'? What do you mean? I never done nuthin'.'

'Sure. Simmer down, John Dog. Don't you see, that woman's an educated lady. She could stir up the Press, the marshals, if you go on the way you're going. We've got a nice little operation started and we don't want anybody to come nosing in. You've a quarter share in the partnership, and only a quarter say. What the majority says goes.'

'Yeah? Well, I ain't never been told what to do, not by some fat, yeller-guts sheriff, nor some pig-bellied meat butcher, nor some hasbeen cap'n in the Union cavalry, if that's what you really was . . . so you listen to me. We do things my way.'

'You're mad,' Newton blustered. 'I tell you you'll ruin everything.'

'I ain't mad, you piece of offal. Don't you call me mad. If it weren't for me you wouldn't have no — '

Cold steel nudged the back of Sundown Jack's neck and a voice whispered, 'Hold it right there, cowboy.'

He started to raise his hands and turned from his crouching position. 'You!' he smiled. 'How you allus manage to git the drop on me?'

'Come on,' she said, taking the Hopkins from his holster. 'You lead the way and don't try no tricks.'

'Aw, come on,' he said. 'I was jest in the middle of a very int'restin' conversation. Put your ear to this.'

'I ain't in the mood. And I guess you've heard enough. Or too much.'

Lou slipped a lasso over his shoulders and jerked it tight. 'Stick out your wrists.'

'Aw, no, you ain't gonna tie me up all night agin? I gotta go warn the boss.'

'Do what I say, or do you want me to yell for help?'

Sundown stuck out his wrists to be tied. 'Anything you say, darlin'.'

She tied him tight and whispered. 'Right, just get moving back to your pinto. And, remember, I'm right behind you.'

★ ★ ★

When they got to the cabin Lou unhitched him and, keeping her gun on him, told him to light the wood in the tin stove and the candle in the bottle.

'You ain't gonna let me freeze to death tonight?' he asked, as he busied himself at the task and soon had the stove burning and a coffee pot bubbling.

'How much do you know?'

'Most everything. Only I can't understand why you helped me git Matthews' hundred head back iffen your ole man bin in with John Dog all this time.'

Lou put her revolver aside, leaned her back against the wall and blew on the hot coffee he passed her. She looked just like a young 'puncher, still in her hat, bandanna, blouse and fringed jacket, the wide batwing chaps over her jeans and high-heeled boots. Her brown eyes had a misty glow in the firelight, and she looked sad and serious, both.

'It's all right for Matthews, he can go back to being a lawman. Or go join that classy woman of his back

192

East. My dad's old. He's teetering on the brink. One more bad winter and he'll be finished.'

'Guess that's a fair enough excuse for going to the bad. But he should beware of falling in with John Dog Crandal. He's jest as likely to git eaten by him. How long you known?'

'Not long. I guess I suspected something was going on. All that about going wolf-huntin'. And then when I saw that he was working hand-in-glove with those killers I was really upset. But what could I do?'

'At least, there's one good thing: they won't hurt you, not with your old man being a partner.'

'I'm not so sure, the looks they give me. More lecherous than yurn.' She gave a smirking grin. 'That's why Dad tries to keep me out of the way. He told me to come out here and stay. That's how I saw you were around.'

'So, you gonna stay with me the night, are you, darlin'?' Sundown lay on the cot and put his feet up. 'There ain' much room in this bunk an' its kinda hard, but — '

'No, it's you who's gonna stay the night. I'm keeping you out of trouble.'

'Thass another thing I don't understand. Why you allus tryin' to protect me?'

Lou stuck her bottom lip out and smirked again. 'I guess I must like you, 'breed.'

'You do? Waal, I'll be gor-swizzled. A purty gal like you, an' a leathery ole 'breed like me.'

'Or maybe it was because Dad said I shouldn't.'

'I'll go fer your first reason.' He filled his pipe and began to light up. 'You sure you know what you're doing?'

Lou took some supplies from her saddle-bags and began to put some fat in the frying pan. 'I know what I'm doing? How about we git some food in our bellies?'

When they had done just that, Lou tossed off her flat-crowned hat, and rolled back on to the bunk beside

Sundown Jack. They rested in silence for a while listening to the stove crackle. She leaned closer against his shoulder and there was a kind of contentment in the cabin.

'All we need to make it real cosy is if I bring my hoss in here.'

'You're real crazy about that ugly, wall-eyed pinto, aincha?' Lou looked up at him. 'You like that snotty piece of goods, Mary Matthews, too, doncha?'

'What makes you say that?'

'I seen the way you look at her. I was in Oglala that day you drove her in.'

'She's a good lady. One the best. Yes, sure, I really like her. Thass true.'

'Some good woman! Runs off at the first sign of trouble. Leaves her man to face it alone.'

'It weren't 'zactly like that.'

'Oh, no?' Lou's voice rose indignantly high. 'You men, 'breeds an' all, you all the same. You let a woman like that pull the wool over your eyes.'

'Do me a favour.' He stared down

at her, his eyes burning, fiercely. 'Don'
keep callin' me 'breed.'

'Well.' She sat apart from him,
bridling up. 'All you want from me
is — well, you know, *that*. You'd be
away the next day. You treat me so
mocking. Contempt, that's what it is,
whereas a fine lady like Mrs So Holy
Matthews you think the sun shines out
of her — '

Sundown Jack put his hand over her
mouth. 'Hush, honey. Don' say things
you don' mean.'

'Well, jest 'cause she can read and
write and knows about all those fal-
de-dah things, music and stuff and
clothes — '

'You tellin' me you cain't read and
write?'

'And how to dance, and talk nice to
folks. No I cain't. So what?'

'Listen, darlin', that stuff don' mean
nuthin' to me. What good is that to us
out here in the woods? You got more
than Missis Matthews got. You know
how to ride, to shoot, to survive in

the wild. Why, you even know how to creep up on me. You better than a dang Injin at that.'

'I sure am,' Lou gave a spluttering laugh. 'You gotta admit that. But what I'm sayin' is — you don't really care for me.'

'Don't I, darlin'? Howja know that?'

He leaned down and touched his mouth to her lips. Hers opened warm and moist to his and her arm curled up and around his neck. 'Well, do you?'

'Jest let me pull them boots and spurs off your purty feet. You'll find out.'

'No, really.'

'Sure I do. I figure we'd make a good team.'

'A good team. You make us sound like dogs. Do you love me, Sundown, that's what I want to know?'

'Ain't that obvious? Sure I do. I'm crazy 'boutcha.'

'Well, why don't you durn well say so?'

13

Christmas Day dawned cold but clear, well below freezing. Matt scouted along the river as far as the Big Bend anxious about the news Sundown Jack had brought him. There was no sign of the outlaws. 'You say there's a dozen of 'em?'

'Thass right, boss. An' they mean business. They plannin' to clean out your herd and you, too, if you ain' careful.'

'Well, they ain't spoiling my Christmas.' Matt grinned, ruefully. 'Let's git back. I gotta git that wild turkey in the oven.'

'Chris'mass!' Sundown took a last look across the river. 'I guess they'll be gittin' sick and crazy on whiskey so they won't bother us. I hope that li'l gal stays outa their way.'

Christmas was the one day of the

year that brought a bitter pang to him. He remembered when he was a small boy hiding in the snowy woods and watching some settler's cabin lit up, the sounds of carousing, the carols and children's laughter. He knew he was an outcast. He did not belong to the white man's world, did not believe in their god. Nor, for that matter, did he believe in the ancient gods of the Sioux, either. He was a 'breed, scorned by the whites, welcomed by the Indians, but not really at one with them. He remembered the time he watched the peaceful cabin in the valley, his longing to go in and be given one of those presents from the tree along with the other children, but knowing it impossible, that he must stay alone. The Christmas season always brought that chill memory back to him. The lady at the mission school told him they must all love their neighbours, but the white folk sure hadn't shown much love to their neighbours, the half-breeds and the Indians.

'Heck!' he muttered. 'What am I

doin' gettin' all starry-eyed 'bout that li'l white gal? Must be goin' loco.'

Matt had given Caleb and Elijah the day off. Well, nobody worked on Christmas Day, apart from tending to the basic chores. He went into his cabin, stamping the snow from his boots. Normally it would have been decorated by Mary with tinsel and coloured lanterns, a tree in the corner. It was bare without her. Still, it didn't mean they couldn't eat. He lit the wood under the wrought-iron stove he had hauled all the way from Cheyenne and shoved the big turkey into it. He sat staring into space for a while, wondering about his family, wondering about John Dog's threats. He began oiling his Remington revolver, and cleaned his Winchester.

It was dark by the time the turkey was basted to perfection. He stepped outside the cabin and looked around at the dark woods and hills. 'What you might call a silent night,' he said, and shattered it by clanging on an iron triangle and hollering over to the bunk-house, 'Come an' git it.'

Caleb ambled over in his ankle-length duster and ten-gallon hat, carrying his carbine under one arm, followed by Elijah. Sundown Jack stepped out and began fondling his pinto in the corral. 'You, too,' Matt shouted. Sundown appeared hesitant, but decided to join them.

'Here you boys, git stuck in,' Matt said. 'Who's gonna have a leg?' He carved off thick slices for them and fetched gravy and greens. 'C'mon, Sundown, you can eat more'n that.'

Sundown flashed a grateful grin at him, proud as a Sioux in his beaded headband. 'First time I ever had Christmas with whiteys.'

When they had finished picking over the turkey and were sprawled, bloated, Matt said, 'Mary would gen'rally have us some plum pudding, but I got something a bit special for you.'

He produced a bottle of fine bourbon.

'Best Kentucky brewed in charred wood. That's my li'l present to you boys. As you know I don't generally imbibe nor allow liquor around the ranch on account of the trouble it generally causes, but I guess we need to relax awhile. I'll just take one glass. How about you, Jack?'

'Sure, boss.' Sundown smacked his lips as he tasted the brew. 'Mighty fine liquor. Yeh!' He downed the glass in one.

'Hey, I want you keepin' a cool head. I'm counting on you to keep a watch out tonight. We'll let these two split the bottle and wake up with sore heads. Here's something else for you, Jack.' He tossed him a pouch of tobacco. 'Merry Christmas, you old son-of-a-gun.'

'Jeez, thanks, boss. I ain't got nuthin' for you. Here!' He untied the beaded headband and passed it across. 'You have. It got luck properties, or so I'se told.'

Sundown's loose hair swung over his

cheeks as he insisted. 'I sure am sorry about your troubles. You bin good to me. I wish I'd shot that John Dog long ago, save you all this.'

Matt smiled, and said, gruffly, 'I'm obliged to you, Jack. This would sure make a nifty hatband. Come on, you two, don't be shy, drink up.'

★ ★ ★

'So, here you are, you li'l whore,' Captain Herb Newton looked like thunder as his daughter stepped into their cabin. 'I'm not surprised you've been skulking out in the woods all day.'

'Why so, Pa?' Lou took her gloves and hat off, and stepped through the sprawled legs of several of the grinning outlaws.

'Vince saw you, saw you comin' out of that cabin in the woods with the 'breed, saw you kissin' him. You'd been with him all night, hadn't you?'

'What if I had, Pa?'

'Whoo!' Slippery whistled. 'She's like that, is she? Fancy ole Sundown Jack gittin' in there. Is it my turn tonight?'

'You shut your mouth,' the old soldier said, rounding angrily on him. 'This ain't none of your business.'

'No, it ain't,' Lou shouted. 'And it ain't none of yours, either. I'm a grown gal.'

'Grown gal!' Newton swung his arm and smacked her across the jaw. 'I'll teach you if you're a grown gal. Get in your bedroom.'

Lou turned her face away sharply from the blow, trying to blink away the tears in her dark eyes. Her pale cheek was reddened by the stinging slap. 'You fool,' she said. 'You shouldn't have done that.'

'Fool?' Herb roared. 'Who you calling fool?'

'Well, you are. Getting mixed up with these scum.'

'Who's she calling scum?' Seedy said.

'Scum and thieves and murderers and you're the same as them. Why'd you have to join them? Why you so damn weak?'

'I did it for you, Daughter. For our livelihood.'

'We coulda survived without this filth.'

'Filth?' John Dog echoed. 'Who the hell she think she is?'

'She's the filth,' Captain Newton sneered, a look of disgust on his features. 'Going with a 'breed. She's brought disgrace on me.'

'Now I know why my mother left.' The pupils of Lou's dark eyes were fixed on him. 'She must have despised you.'

'Left?' John Dog said. 'I thought you said she was dead?'

'What difference,' Newton shrugged, tugging at his white moustache. 'She's dead to me.'

'She ran off with a peddler man. And I don't blame her.'

'She was a whore. And you've turned out like her. A lousy 'breed, eh? He had his fun, did he? Well, that's the last fun he'll ever have with a white gal. Saddle up, boys. I'm gonna go kill me that 'breed.'

'No,' Lou shouted, and her hand went to her revolver. But John Dog was there before her, slipping it from the holster, grinning at her. 'No, you don't, sweetie. You git in your bedroom like your daddy says. Me an' you gonna git together when we get back.'

'That's enough of that talk, Crandal. Get in your room, girl.'

Crandal got her by the shoulders and thrust her through the door into the windowless back room. Newton quickly bolted and locked it with a big padlock. The captain picked up his rifle and shouted, 'Remember! The 'breed's mine.'

★ ★ ★

Matt Matthews had found some cheese, nuts and biscuits for the men, he and Sundown smiling at Caleb's drunken efforts to sing, 'I was a good li'l gal 'fore I met you . . . ' when he heard the crackling sound of burning and saw a red glow flickering through the window from outside. His face set in anguish as he gasped, 'My God! It's the stables.'

'What?' Caleb staggered to the door and reached for the latch.

'Don't open — ' Matt shouted, dousing the lamp.

But it was too late. The door was opened and Caleb uttered a croaking cry like a turkey gobble as a slug hurtled into his throat. He retraced his footsteps and collapsed on the wooden floor, his eyes staring, vacantly.

'He's dead,' Elijah said.

They heard the horsemen whooping and riding back and forth, tar brands in their hands. They were setting light to the barn and outhouses. One hurled a brand on to the bunkhouse. And there was John Dog's shrill voice yelling, 'Come out, Sundown Jack. You been a naughty boy. The Cap'n wants a word with you.'

Sundown smashed out the cabin

window with his carbine, and was down on one knee, poking the barrel through. He fired, jerking the lever three times. 'Cain't make out who's who, but I got one of 'em.'

'We gotta get to the stable,' Matt gritted out. 'There's a mare and foal in there.'

'Out back through the cellar,' Sundown cried. 'I'll cover you. Go with him Elijah.'

Sundown fed another slug into the breech of the carbine, and took careful aim as one of the riders galloped by. There was a flash of flame. It was the last shot that rider ever took. He was dragged away, one foot caught in his stirrup.

Matt and Elijah climbed from the unroofed cellar. 'Git down behind that horse trough, Elijah. It's every man for hisself. They ain't gonna give us no mercy.'

Matt raced across to the stable, dodging through swirling hooves and gunfire, hauling the barn doors open.

He recoiled at the blast of hot smoke from the burning hay, and, holding a hand over his face ventured in. Chickens ran squawking out between his boots and, foolishly, ran back in again.

Matt could hardly see or breathe through the dancing orange flames, the burning heat, the choking smoke. He heard the horses' screams of terror, and began unbolting stalls, dragging the horses out. They kicked out with fear not wanting to go. He took off his jacket, wrapped it around their heads, and led them to the door. A slap on their haunches and they went racing away. He whacked the cows with a stick, forced them to make a run for it. Where was the mare and foal? At the farthest end. He ducked back as a burning beam crashed down. The whole place was an inferno. Matt hesitated, glancing back at the door from which smoke was pouring. 'Damn it,' he said. 'I'm not leaving them.'

He dunked a gunny sack in a bucket of water, and went blindly forward. He found the mare, wrapped it around her head and led her out, dragging the foal along with him. There were more horses in there but there was no way he could get back in.

Back outside he stood coughing on smoke, trying to see through the tears in his sore eyes. They had thrown tar brands on the cabin roof and it was going up, in spite of its layer of snow. When Matt's eyes cleared he saw Sundown Jack dash from the cabin, firing his revolver as he did so. The dark and shadowy riders in their tall hats and long coats sent a volley of lead his way. Miraculously he escaped death, but a bullet in the leg brought him down. Another hit the Hopkins from his hand.

'He's mine!' a husky voice shouted and Matt saw Captain Herb Newton in his Union garb ride forward, his rifle aimed at the fallen Jack.

Matt's Remington came from his

holster in a smooth, fluid action. He raised his arm, aimed, fired. The shot caught Newton in the side, beneath his arm. He turned, a grimace of frustration and horror on his face, and toppled from his horse.

Matt joined Elijah behind the horse trough as Jack lay on the ground in front of the cabin. Matt picked his shots, and two men went spinning, one pierced through the brain, the other the abdomen. Sundown managed to wriggle away into the darkness as bullets thudded into the woodwork about him.

What horsemen remained were having second thoughts and backing away in a knot together. John Dog! Surely that was him, the tall, ragged, bearded and mean-looking one in the middle. The man who had caused all this mayhem. Matt took careful aim with the Remington, squeezed the trigger, but there was only an empty click. He was out of lead. 'Shee-it!' he groaned.

Matt lay back to reload with bullets

211

from his gunbelt and there was a momentary lapse in hostilities. The cabin roof had caught and was burning wildly, casting its fiery glow all around.

John Dog pointed his revolver and howled at them, 'I'll be back, Matthews. And for you, Sundown. I'll be back.' With that he led his men at a gallop out of the ranch.

Matt stood and aimed a last shot after them, and looked about him at the havoc caused, awestruck.

'You know, I think that fellow's insane,' he said, but gave a grin of relief that they, at least, were still alive.

'He's crazy,' Elijah said, his eyes wild. 'They all are. They must be. Why'd they do this?'

Matt shook his head, sadly. 'There ain't no way we're going to save the cabin. Maybe they jest like hurtin' people.'

'Caleb's in there.'

'Yeah. There ain't gonna be much left of him. Poor old guy. He was brave to the end.'

'At least he died with whiskey inside him and his boots on. He allus said he'd hate to end a cripple and down-and-out.'

Matt went to look at Sundown's leg. 'How is it?'

Jack shook his head, his hair hanging loose to his shoulders. 'It ain't so bad.'

Matt pulled apart the bloody buckskin. 'Gone clean through the flesh. You're lucky. Don't think it's caught the bone.' He pulled off his bandanna and wrapped it around the wound, tightly. 'We'll get you over to the bunkhouse. Thank God that sod roof wouldn't burn. I better bring the foal in, too.'

He hoisted Sundown up to lean on his shoulder and together they looked down at the fallen Herb Newton. 'I owed him that,' Matt said. 'I never did like the man.' He leaned down and pulled the scarlet Apache headband away from the grey hair. The flamelight showed a large 'C' branded on Newton's forehead.

'I wondered why he never took that off,' Matt said. 'Looks like he weren't such a hero in the war, after all. They branded him as a coward. He would have been ignominiously discharged.'

'Maybe,' Sundown said, 'we shouldn't tell Lou that. I'm sure glad *you* kilt him.'

'C'mon, young fellow, we got to get you over to the bunkhouse, take a look at that leg.'

'What we gonna do with all these other dead uns?' Elijah asked.

'I don't know,' Matt said. 'And to tell you the truth I don't really care. I hope their souls rot in Hell.'

14

He did not think of doing any burying. The frozen men and the burned animals could wait. In the first light of dawn Matthews rode out. He looked up at the grey sky and did not like what he saw. The snow had ceased but he scented and felt against his face a soft warm wind, a chinook. It did not bode well. It would partly melt the snow into a thick mushy slush. If such a thaw continued all well and good, but at that low point of winter it was hardly likely. He knew the worst was yet to come.

Sundown Jack had wanted to go with him, but he could hardly put any pressure on the torn ligament of his leg. And the bullet-cut across his gunhand was none too good. 'You gotta rest up. I don't need you. You would only slow me up,' Matt grunted. 'This is my fight.'

He had told Elijah to go inform Luke Hanlon, the sheriff, about what had happened. He saw the young cowboy's gulp of relief. Matt was set on a possibly suicidal mission. He did not know how many men he would have to face. No reason to get another innocent man killed. As for himself, any fear that lurked in him was offset by a grim determination to have a showdown, once and for all, whatever the cost. The shock of his burned-to-the-ground cabin home and stables had rendered him coldly emotionless. He rode on through the snowy mountains like a relentless automaton following the trail of the men. He came across a few knots of cattle, but most were so skeletal thin and weak even the rustlers would not have bothered stealing them. If another blizzard came it was doubtful if many would survive.

The sun had appeared through the misty clouds assisting the meltdown. It, at least, helped him to plough his horse through the ice on the river's edge and wade across the bitterly cold stream. The way Matt felt he was impervious to sensations of cold or hunger, his mind set on one target — catching up. The Newton spread was deserted, or seemed to be. The rancher swung down from his horse and approached with caution. It looked like Herb's men, the ones who hadn't been killed, had joined forces with the outlaws. An echoing clangour from the wagon shed drew him over. It was Dan, the old craftsman in his leather apron, hard at work making a coffin. 'Howdy,' he muttered, through the nails he held in his teeth.

'Howdy. S'pose you heard Herb's dead?'

'Yeah.' Dan carried on, impassively. 'They've gawn. He should never have got mixed up with them. I figure he'd want to be buried here. You got the body?'

'Nope. You kin go git it if you want. Where's Lou?'

'She's gawn. I heard her banging on

her room door so I let her out. I told her to go hide herself 'fore they got back. She looked pretty scared. Hightailed it up towards Medicine Creek.'

'Good. She's only a kid. Them varmints would have been just as like to rape and kill her.'

'That's what I figured.'

'One thing's for sure,' Matt said, eyeing the quality of the planed wood. 'You'll never be out of a job. Guess you'll be sold as part of the ranch.'

'You reckon it'll be sold?'

'Sure, Miss Lou couldn't run it herself.'

'You headin' on? Make yourself a coffee and a bite to eat 'fore you go.'

'Yeah, maybe I will. I'll give my bronc a bucket of oats. We're gonna need all the energy we can get. Looks to me like it might freeze tonight.'

★ ★ ★

It didn't just freeze: overnight the temperature went down like a toboggan.

When Matt woke from a fitful sleep camped along the estuary of the Little Snake it was as if freezing arrows were piercing his lungs. The cold seemed to clamp a tight iron band around his brow, numbing his hands and feet and brain. He dimly guessed as he fed his fire that it must already be forty degrees below zero and falling fast. Overnight the soft warm chinook had turned into a razoring wind. The mushy slush on the ground had become solid. There was no question of even horses being able to paw through for food, let alone cattle. He had to use an axe to hack through six inches of ice at the river edge for his bronc to drink and to get some for his kettle. The chinook, followed by this freeze, would turn the whole of the western plains into a solid plate of ice. It was the worst possible scenario for cattlemen.

When he had made some sort of breakfast Matt warmed the horse's bit under his arm so it would not burn its mouth, cinched the saddle tight, and hauled himself aboard. He pulled his bandanna up over his face against a wind that tore tears from his eye corners, and kicked his horse forward. The beast slipped and slithered on the treacherous ice. The rancher was in constant danger of falling and breaking his neck, but he spurred on, his mind set, a cold emptiness in his chest. And in his heart.

★ ★ ★

'You missed me, sweetheart?' John Dog Crandal stomped into the Ace-in-the-Hole brushing snow from his ragged and dirt-engrained clothes, kicking ice from his worn boots.

'No I ain't,' Hetty L'Amour said.

John Dog gave a roar of laughter, swaggered towards her, the rowels of his spurs clinking on the wooden floor, and gripped her by the hair at the scruff of her neck, jerking her head back. Hetty stared up at him, defiantly, her nostrils twitching at his stale aroma, recoiling from his grinning teeth and manic eyes. 'If you ever took a bath it might help.'

John Dog bit savagely into her scarlet, cupid-bow lips, making her yelp with pain, and he snarled, 'Teach ya to talk to me like that. Git up to your room. I'll be up to see to you in a while.'

When Hetty demurred and turned away, John Dog caught hold of her and thrust her towards the stairs. 'You do what I say.'

The girl narrowed her dark-outlined green eyes and glowered at him, a mixture of fear and anger seething in her as she backed away up the stairs to the landing. 'I hate you,' she hissed.

Crandal laughed, slapped soldier Finnegan on the shoulder, and went behind the bar. He jerked the cork off a bottle of whiskey and took it by the neck, his Adam's apple bobbing as he swallowed the fiery liquid down. He gave a gasp and passed the bottle across. 'That's the way I like my wimmin, like my liquor, with fire in 'em. I'll make that bitch squeal.'

'Sure you will,' Finnegan said, taking a swig. 'What is it you like best, killing a man or hurting some woman or creature that can't defend itself?'

'What's it to you, Snake Eyes? You goin' all preacher on me? Gimme that bottle.' He snatched it back. 'What's the matter with everybody? What is this, a wake, or somethun'? Drinks all along for the boys, 'keep. Piano-player start pumpin'. You gals git up there an' dance. Where is everybody? Let's show 'em we're here for a good time. Start them roulette wheels turning.'

The pianist began an uncertain tinny and off-tune, melody. The girls, in their gaudy paint, skimpy dresses and stockings scrambled up on the stage and started prancing about like mechanical dolls, and John Dog scowled, 'That's better.' He turned back to Finnegan. 'You think I shouldn't git a thrill from killing a man, from beating up on a whore? Why not? It excites me. You got any objection?'

'And burning a decent man's home down about his ears, that excites you, too?'

'Sure,' Crandal roared. 'Why not?'

'Well, it ain't my idea of fun. So I figure you'd better pay me what you owe me and I'll be moving on.'

'Nobody moves out on me unless it's feet first. You know too much.'

'Is that so?' Snake Eyes said. 'Well, in my opinion, Crandal, you're playing with dynamite. What you did to that rancher was a fool thing to do.'

Ferguson came storming in. 'What did you do? Burn Matthews down? I've just heard. That sure was a fool thing, Crandal. How many men you lose?'

'Aw, half a dozen. So what? We can soon recruit a few more. There's plenty drifters about. What you belly-aching about, Abe? Cap'n Newton's dead. He was our partner, weren't he? So now his ranch belongs to us.'

'It ain't as simple as that.' Ferguson tried to pull in his big stomach and push out his chest. 'What about his daughter?'

'Don't worry. We won't have no trouble with her. And pretty soon we could own Matthews' land, as well. We'll be one of the biggest cattle companies in Wyoming once we've put him out of business.'

'You're going about it the wrong way. I've told you before. We gotta look like we're biding by the law.'

'Come on, quit whining. There ain't no law in Troublesome. You should know that. Come on in, gents,' he called, to some men pushing through the swing doors. 'What's your pizen? Something to keep out the cold? Toss some more logs on that durn stove. I ain't never known such down-belows. We was lucky we didn't all freeze to death on the trail. Cold to suck the life out of a man.'

'I still don't like it. Matthews used to be a lawman. Me and Murphy — '

'Here y'are, Abe, have a bottle. Go git in a game of poker. Me,

I got a li'l gal to see to upstairs. That Hetty bin gittin' cheeky.' He returned his attention to Finnegan. 'If you thinkin' of quittin' you better think again. Where you gonna go, Snake Eyes? Where you gonna find a set-up like this? All the liquor you can drink? Come on, me, you, Slippery and Seedy, we're a team.'

15

Shutters banged madly, tumbleweed went rolling through the frozen Main Street of Troublesome, the clapboard buildings trembled and groaned as the blizzard raged and howled across the plains. Folks ran for cover or tried to hammer boards across their windows. Horses and dogs were left to their own devices, whinnying and howling their fear. A stray longhorn bull went careering down the street, dipping its vicious horns, its tail up. And Abe Henderson stood on the wooden broadwalk outside the sheriff's office and gave a whistle of awe. Through the flailing snow he could see a dark figure riding his horse into town, silhouetted against a deep purple sky.

'What's he doing here?' He loosened his Colt .45 in its holster and thumbed back the hammer. 'He sure got a nerve.'

Henderson went hurrying across to the saloon, giving a squawking curse as he slipped and landed on his fat backside in the snow. He scrambled up and, giving a fearful glance back at the rider, climbed on to the sidewalk and pushed through the batwing doors. 'Crandal! He's here.'

John Dog was sitting at a table with his cronies having breakfast of coffee and biscuits and counting through the silver and paper dollars of the night's takings. 'Who?'

'You know who. Matthews.'

John Dog narrowed his eyes and stopped mid-count. 'Matthews? What's he want?'

'What you think he wants?'

John Dog licked his thin lips and snarled, 'In that case get back to your office you fat fool. Keep him talking. When we come outa the Ace and he walks towards us, you shoot him in the back.'

Abe's jaw dropped. 'I ain't got no fight with him.'

'You do as I say. You're in this with us. It's easy. Jest shoot him in the back an' we'll do the rest. We gotta put him down, Abe. It's the only way.'

Henderson stared. His eyes bulging, and, mouth still gawping, he hurried out of the door.

John Dog pulled his new long-barrelled Whitney .36 he had bought from the town gunshop. 'I bin wantin' to try this out,' he grinned, checking the cylinder was full. He stuffed a cardboard box of bullets into his coat pocket and got to his feet.

'Seedy you git up in one of the gal's rooms at the window. Slippery, you go out the back and git positioned in the livery loft. Take your rifle.'

'We'll get him,' Seedy laughed, moving away up the stairs. 'He ain't got a snowball's chance in hell.'

John Dog buttoned his bullet-scarred frock coat and went to the bar. He poured himself a tumbler of whiskey and frowned at Finnegan. 'You with us, Sarge?'

The ex-quartermaster poured himself a shot and tossed it back. He tugged his forage cap down tight, gripped his carbine and grunted. 'Looks like it's the way it's got to be.'

'Be careful, boys,' John Dog said to five assorted mean-eyed *hombres* he had put on the payroll. 'Soon as I say, we all start shootin' and cut him to ribbons.'

'Thass what you payin' us fer,' one of Herb Newton's former range-riders growled, cinching his gunbelt. 'I got a score to settle for the cap'n.'

'The boys should be in position by now. Let's go.'

John Dog led his men out onto the sidewalk of the Ace-in-the-Hole. The morning was as dark as dusk and the bitter wind tore at their hats and coats as they fanned out in readiness. Through the driving snowflakes John Dog could make out a man in a fur coat and Stetson hitching his horse outside the sheriff's office. He was talking to Ferguson.

229

'You cain't take the law into your own hands, Matt,' Ferguson said. 'You best git out.'

'What law?' Matt sneered. 'Where's John Dog?'

'Over there. I'll back you, Matt, if there's trouble.'

'Sure.'

'Matthews,' John Dog hollered against the wind. 'It's me an' you. Come out here.'

Matt pulled back the bear coat and turned towards them. He patted the heavy Remington in his holster and began to march across. 'You're the one I'm looking for, Crandal,' he shouted.

'Come and get me.' John Dog glanced at his men and winked. 'I'll fight you fair and square,' he yelled.

'You other men, put away your guns. I got no argument with you. This is between me and him.'

Crandal gave a wild grin and stepped forward. 'He must be joking. Ready, boys?'

Matt could see the six of them lined

up, their guns at the ready, dark as statues. He knew he hadn't got a chance against such odds, but there was no going back.

'Come out here into the open, Crandal, you piece of filth. Or are you scared?'

'Scared of you,' Crandal screamed. 'You crazy? You gonna die.' He jumped down from the side-walk and crouched at the ready, his gun still in his belt.

People sensed trouble and hurried to get off the street as Matt started forward again. Tongues of snow came snaking along the dark ice down the wide street and, looking along, Crandal saw another horseman riding in. A short, shaggy pinto carrying a hunch-shouldered man in a tall black hat. Something made him shudder at the sight, as if someone had stepped on his grave. 'The 'breed!'

Abe Ferguson pulled out his Colt, raised it, stepping forward, cocked the hammer and fired but, as he did so, lost his footing on the mirror-like surface of the boardwalk. His bullet whistled past Matt's ear.

The rancher spun around, saw Abe regaining his feet, with his gun drawn, and his Remington was out. It barked out lead and the fat sheriff went flying back to land against his office door. He stared with anguish at the rancher as blood trickled from his lips.

Matt, himself, felt the dizziness coming over him. He slipped and landed in a deep rut of ice as the men on the porch, led by John Dog, sent a fusillade of shots ringing and chipping about him. He peered across the ice through a hail of lead and tried to concentrate, return fire.

Sundown Jack kneed his pinto carefully forward. He had seen a puff of black powder smoke from the livery loft. There was a shadowy figure up there aiming a rifle at Matt. He rode up close and took him out with a straight-armed shot from his new Hawkins .44. Slippery Williams pitched forward, tumbling from the loft to land flat on his back in the street. Sundown finished him with another shot and turned his attention to the men outside the Ace-in-the-Hole.

Two of Crandal's men gave cries of pain and surprise as bullets cut through their flesh. They fell, one dead, one writhing in agony. John Dog's eyes rolled, wildly. He wasn't prepared for this. He tried to scramble back up onto the sidewalk as another bullet spurted ice by his toes. It had come from another direction, and he looked along with alarm to the other end of the street. He saw through the gloom of flying snowflakes a young cowboy on a horse approaching, a rifle at shoulder — or was it a girl? Lou! He aimed his Whitney .36 carefully to kill her, and gritted his teeth as he squeezed a slug out.

Lou leapt from her horse as John Dog's lead whined past her head. There was the crack of a rifle from an upstairs window of the Ace, the bullet ripping through the sleeve of her fringed buckskin. Two narrow escapes! She dived for cover behind a wagon wheel and joined in the fray.

The cylinder of Matt's Remington was hot in his hand as he lay and reloaded. The dizzy spell had passed and he tried to concentrate on the task amid bullets that buzzed and spat about him like bees.

He got to his feet and started towards the saloon again, aiming at the tall man with a face like a grinning dog. But Crandal was backing away, getting behind his men, pushing them to the front, using them as a shield. Up at the saloon window, Seedy Smith peeped out and took a bead with his rifle on Matthews' heart. He couldn't miss. But, as he did so, a small calibre bullet thudded into his back. He gave a gasp of shock and twisted around falling to the bedroom floor.

Hetty L'Amour stood, her face tense, a little derringer two-shot in her fist. She ejected the spent case as the dying Smith struggled to raise his rifle, to jerk down the lever, feed lead into the breech, aim at her. 'You — ' he said, and slumped lifeless as the singer girl's second shot hit him in the heart.

'That was for my friend Sally,' she whispered.

As yet another *hombre* collapsed wounded before him, Crandal dodged, ducked and winced with fear as Matthews, Sundown Jack on his pinto, and the girl, Lou, closed in, their bullets hammering into the wooden wall, making splinters fly. 'Hell take this,' Finnegan said, and threw his gun away, raising his hands high. Another man beside him, out of lead, did the same.

John Dog's grey eyes glittered with alarm as his men died or deserted him and he backed away into the saloon. He grabbed at the dollars and silver on the table, stuffing them into his pockets, picked up his carbine, took a shot through the batwing doors to keep back whoever was out there, and turned to dash out the back entrance where he had a horse tethered.

'Hold it, Crandal!' a girl's voice spat out from the landing. He looked up with surprise to see Hetty standing there. She had Seedy Smith's rifle in her hands. 'You don't think I'd let you go?'

'Don' be a fool, Hetty. Come with me. I'm rich.' He jerked his carbine up and fired as her rifle bullet exploded through his chest, sending him tumbling back to the bar.

'You lousy bitch.' He hung on to the bar, met her eyes, and tried for another shot. Hetty jerked the lever and fired again. And again, tears in her eyes. John Dog Crandal twisted and danced in agony before crashing to the floor. Hetty had pumped seven bullets into him before Matthews got there. Crandal's blood was already flowing across the boards.

'It's OK.' Matt raised his hand. 'Quit firin'. He's dead.'

Hetty didn't stop ploughing bullets into John Dog until the rifle's sixteen were spent. She threw the weapon clattering aside and descended the stairs to peer at him. 'The rat,' she said, and spat at him. Then she burst into sobs and Matt hugged her to his bearskin, soothing her. 'It's all over now, gal.'

Sundown Jack burst through the batwing doors on his pinto, with a clatter of hooves, sending tables and glasses crashing, his carbine at the ready. In the powdersmoke and candlelight his dark eyes glistened beneath his hat. 'Everybody done?'

Matt nodded. 'Everybody done. Thought I told you to stay at home.'

'Aw.' Jack gave a grimace of pain as he slithered from his saddle and hobbled, stiff-legged to the bar. He poured himself a glass of whiskey. 'Figured you might need some help.'

'I weren't 'spectin' to come through,' Matt said, and stared at the blood-riddled figure on the ground. 'First time I seen him up close.'

Lou led Finnegan and two injured 'punchers in at the point of a rifle.

'What we gonna do with these specimens?' she said.

'Howdy, Snake Eyes,' Jack grinned. 'Guess you backed the wrong side.'

'Sure, I did so, indeed. Have you got a drop of that before they string us high?'

Sundown pushed the bottle across. 'Help yourself. You weren't no friend of John Dog. I know that. Neither us liked the way he acted, specially to that ferryman's missis. You shoulda got out then.'

'Give the gal a drink,' Matt said, sitting Hetty down. He went up and took a look at the injured gunmen, one nursing a bloody shoulder, the other a shattered finger. And sized-up Finnegan. 'Lock 'em up in Abe's cooler. I wouldn't hang a dog in this weather.'

'What we gonna do now?' Lou asked.

'Honey, we gonna take a nice li'l room upstairs.' Sundown hugged her to him in one arm. 'Ain' no use goin'

nowhere 'til this blizzard's blown itself
out. An'I guess that'll be a few days.'

'We ain' married.'

'We kin soon fix that. Must be a
preacher in this town.'

16

The temperature plummeted and kept on falling to 50° below zero. The blizzards raged across Wyoming building up great drifts, half-burying cabins, rattling shutters and stovepipes. Not many people ventured out. They hung around their stoves. Sundown and Lou stayed mainly in bed. For them it was a blissful honeymoon. In mid-January the way-belows broke and there was a respite from the tireless blizzards. The sun even showed. 'I never thought a minus-thirty wind would feel balmy,' Sundown grinned, poking his nose out of the door.

Matthews, who had moved into the bunkhouse with Elijah, began rebuilding the cabin around the iron stove. They made a lean-to for the milch cows. When he searched out on his horse along the coulées and

240

riverbank he wondered why he was bothering. His face became gaunt and strained as he counted the heaped carcasses of his cattle.

Eventually, warmth returned to the land. The ice along the river edges began to melt and break away. The spruce trees began to shed their heavy layers of snow, and the thick load on the bunkhouse roof began to drip and slide. Matt could hear the elks bugling their mating calls along the valley. The prairie grouse began to warble and display. The sun soared higher and the grass showed, yellowed by the snow. It would soon green over. It should have been a time of joy, but the round-ups of the spring of 1887 were the quietest on record. No joking, singing, or horseplay. Just men counting the dead. Matt was not the only one to suffer, he knew that. In large parts of Wyoming eighty per cent of cattle were killed.

It was not until after the round-ups the appalling size of the catastrophe to cattlemen was detailed in the *Wyoming Citizen*. Great firms like the Continental Land and Cattle Company had been reduced to practically nothing. Swan Land and Cattle, a Scottish outfit, which had had 5,500 three-year-old steers ready for market found only one hundred of these alive. Companies were crippled everywhere, large and small. Among those who disappeared from the range after the disaster was the cowboy president, Theodore Roosevelt. He left the bones of his cattle behind him north of Medora. Men had never known the like of it before.

'I'm thinking of packing up and going back to being a lawman,' Matt told Luke Hanlon, after they had sorted out the burials and paperwork of the John Dog mayhem. 'At least it's a regular wage in the pocket.'

'Waal, it's sure quieter since Hetty put Crandal down,' Luke said. 'They could do with a good man in Troublesome.'

'Mebbe I'll put myself forward. I

ain't got fifty dollars to my name.'

On a fine spring morning a few days later Matt was riding towards Oglala to see about this when he saw a buggy coming towards him across the plain going at a good trot. He saw, as they neared, that a young woman was holding the reins, the sun gleaming on her golden hair. His heart began to soar like a meadowlark when he made out a yellow-haired boy by her side. He put spurs to his bronc and galloped towards them, the wind bending back the brim of his hat, excitement and exhilaration pounding through him with every thud of the flying hooves.

'Pa!' Jed yelled, and leaped on to his horse behind him as they drew alongside.

Mary's eyes sparkled as blue as the sky and there was a newfound warmth in her smile. A little girl, Lucy Johnson, was sitting between her knees. 'Didn't you get my telegraph?' she called.

'Nope. The line's been down for weeks. Who's this?'

243

'She's your new daughter. She's got no other kin. We've come back.' Mary's smile faltered as she watched his face. 'Is that OK?'

'Sure 'tis.' He leaned over and gripped her hand, feeling shy and awkward. 'Only — '

'Only what?'

'Only, it's bin bad. We ain't got no ranch no more. I'm broke, Mary. Wiped out, like a lot more. You musta read.'

'But you still own the land, don't you?'

'Sure, homesteader's rights. But what cattle's left ain't worth a hill of beans.'

'You've got men, haven't you, Matt?'

'Only Elijah. Caleb's dead, burned with our cabin. It's bin bad, I said. It's all through now, though.'

'I'm sorry about Caleb, about — '

'Thass all right, Mary. Sundown Jack's wed to Lou and running the Newton spread. They got a fella called Finnegan helping them. He's a rough diamond, but seems OK.'

'Well, if Sundown Jack and Lou can do it, so can we.'

'Mary, you don't understand. I'm through! Our home's burned down. I hardly got enough to pay Elijah off.'

'I've got money.' She smiled, radiantly. 'The sale of the house. Dad's books. We've got plenty to restock.'

'Yeah,' Jed chimed in. 'Gramps is a celebrity.'

'I don't want your money, Mary. I didn't marry you for that.'

'Don't be so old-fashioned. What's mine is yours. Anyway, it's my father's really. We're partners from now on. If we all pull together we'll get through.'

'Sure we will,' Jed yelled. 'Isn't it great to be back, Ma?'

'Mm,' she smiled. 'Just smell this fresh air. So, come on, partner, turn that hoss around and let's go home. I'm dying to get the kettle on.'

Matt grinned and set the horse at a jog along beside her, the boy clinging to his waist. 'It sure is good to have you back,' he said.

'Hey, Pa, maybe we could go into partnership with Sundown Jack and Lou! Build up one big spread?'

'Yes,' Mary said. 'Us Westerners have got to start being more businesslike. The old feuding days are over.'

'Yup. Maybe they are,' Matt grunted. 'Maybe we could.'

THE END

Other titles in the
Linford Western Library

THE CROOKED SHERIFF
John Dyson

Black Pete Bowen quit Texas with a burning hatred of men who try to take the law into their own hands. But he discovers that things aren't much different in the silver mountains of Arizona.

THEY'LL HANG BILLY
FOR SURE:
Larry & Stretch
Marshall Grover

Billy Reese, the West's most notorious desperado, was to stand trial. From all compass points came the curious and the greedy, the riff-raff of the frontier. Suddenly, a crazed killer was on the loose — but the Texas Trouble-Shooters were there, girding their loins for action.

RIDERS OF RIFLE RANGE
Wade Hamilton
Veterinarian Jeff Jones did not like open warfare — but it was there on Scrub Pine grass. When he diagnosed a sick bull on the Endicott ranch as having the contagious blackleg disease, he got involved in the warfare — whether he liked it or not!

BEAR PAW
Nevada Carter
Austin Dailey traded two cows to a pair of Indians for a bay horse, which subsequently disappeared. Tracks led to a secret hideout of fugitive Indians — and cattle thieves. Indians and stockmen co-operated against the rustlers. But it was Pale Woman who acted as interpreter between her people and the rangemen.

THE WEST WITCH
Lance Howard

Detective Quinton Hilcrest journeys west, seeking the Black Hood Bandits' lost fortune. Within hours of arriving in Hags Bend, he is fighting for his life, ensnared with a beautiful outcast the town claims is a witch! Can he save the young woman from the angry mob?

GUNS OF THE PONY EXPRESS
T. M. Dolan

Rich Zennor joined the Pony Express venture at the start, as second-in-command to tough Denning Hartman. But Zennor had the problems of Hartman believing that they had crossed trails in the past, and the fact that he was strongly attached to Hartman's Indian girl, Conchita.

BLACK JO OF THE PECOS
Jeff Blaine

Nobody knew where Black Josephine Callard came from or whither she returned. Deputy U.S. Marshal Frank Haggard would have to exercise all his cunning and ability to stay alive before he could defeat her highly successful gang and solve the mystery.

RIDE FOR YOUR LIFE
Johnny Mack Bride

They rode west, hoping for a new start. Then they met another broken-down casualty of war, and he had a plan that might deliver them from despair. But the only men who would attempt it would be the truly brave — or the desperate. They were both.